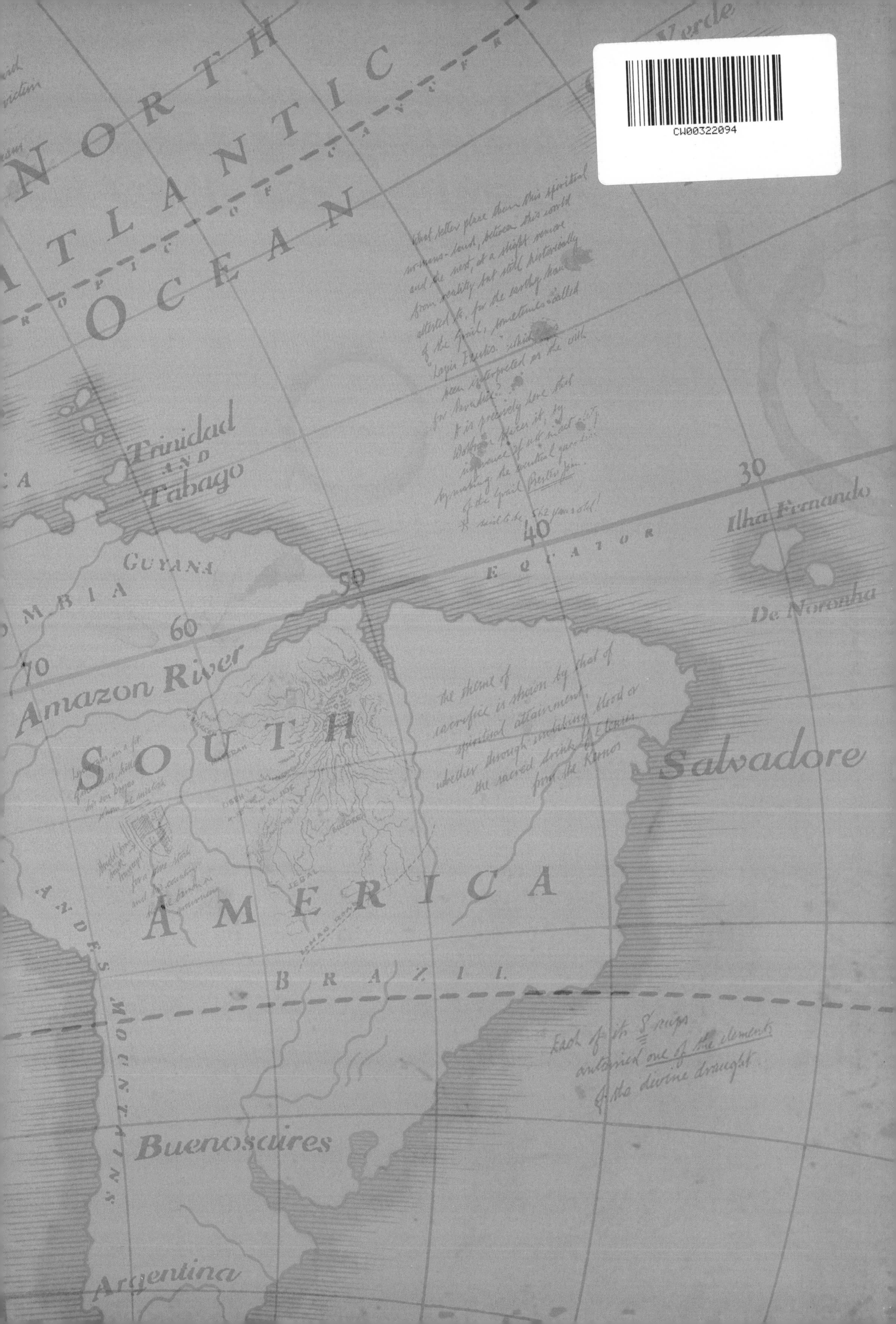

NORTH

ATLANTIC

OCEAN

TROPIC OF CANCER

Verde

Trinidad AND Tabago

GUYANA

COLOMBIA

Amazon River

70 60 50 40 30

EQUATOR

Ilha Fernando

De Noronha

SOUTH

AMERICA

BRAZIL

ANDES MOUNTAINS

Salvadore

Buenosaires

Argentina

CONTENTS

Published 2009. Published by Pedigree Books Ltd, Beech Hill House, Walnut Gardens, Exeter, Devon EX4 4DH. Email: books@pedigreegroup.co.uk. www.pedigreebooks.com

INDIANA JONES
TIMELINE

1899	Henry 'Indiana' Jones Junior is born
1912	Indiana's mother dies
1916	Quits School Joins the Mexican Revolution Fights in the First World War
1918	Attends the University of Chicago, studies archaeology under Professor Abner Ravenwood and alongside Henry Oxley
1922	Graduates and goes to study linguistics in Paris, France
1925	Starts his first teaching job at London University, England
1926	Joins Abner Ravenwood on a dig in Jerusalem Has a brief romance with Abner's daughter, Marion
1935	Foils a plot by the Thuggee cult to steal the Sankara stones
1936	Asked by the US Government to find the Ark of the Covenant Is reunited with Marion Ravenwood

1937	Leaves Marion shortly before their wedding
1938	Finds the Holy Grail, with the help of his father, Henry Jones Senior
1939-1945	Fights in the Second World War Spies for the Office of Strategic Services Meets M16 agent George 'Mac' McHale
1957	Foils the plot of Soviets searching for the Crystal Skull of Akator Marries his former fiancée Marion Ravenwood Discovers Mutt Williams is his son

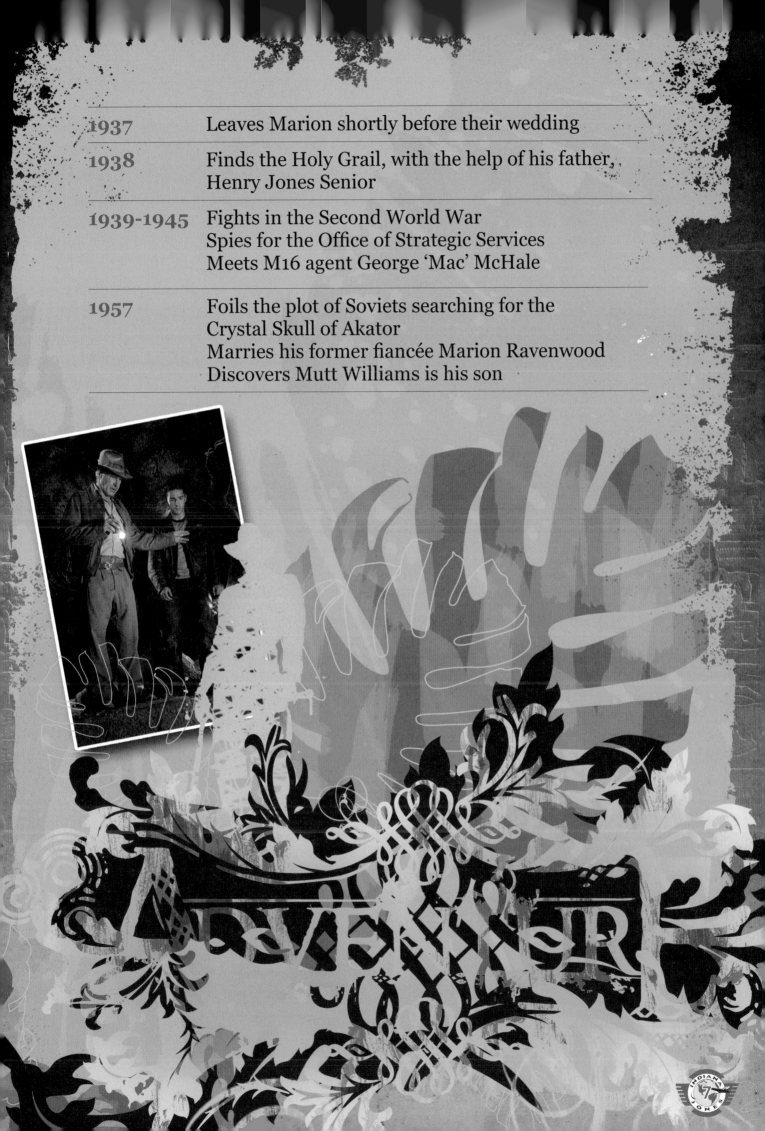

INDIANA JONES™

[PROFILE]

Professor, war hero, archaeologist and adventurer, Doctor Henry 'Indiana' Jones is a true American hero. His early life was spent eagerly pursuing artefacts and this often got him into trouble.

Growing up, the young Jones struggled to gain the attention and affection he craved from his father, Professor Henry Jones Senior. Professor Jones was completely consumed with his work, researching the legend of the Holy Grail, and remained shut away in his study. Indy's mother sadly died when he was just a boy. Indiana left school at age 17 to travel the world, becoming embroiled in the Mexican Revolution and the First World War.

Indy travels the world protecting history and ensuring that ancient finds are preserved in museums whilst also searching for fortune and glory.

Indy is at the forefront of archaeology and one of the brightest academic minds in America. He is certainly not afraid to get his hands dirty and puts his life on the line during his adventures. He has the gift of the gab and is a real hit with the ladies, usually getting the girl no matter how much he antagonises her along the way!

Over the years Indy has discovered some of the world's most valuable and intriguing treasures. He has met many important historical figures, including Adolf Hitler, has fought in both World Wars and has worked for intelligence agencies all over the globe.

His first love will always be archaeology, and he lectures young students on ancient history at Marshall College while travelling the world seeking out rare artefacts, investigating legends and making sure that the power, riches and traditions of these sacred treasures are kept out of evil hands.

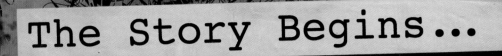

RAIDERS OF THE LOST ARK

Marion
Ravenwood

One of Indy's first girlfriends and probably the love of his life, Marion Ravenwood shares a lot of Dr Jones' character traits. She is feisty, stubborn and doesn't know when to shut up! But her bravery, determination and almost unwavering support for Indy means he would always rather have her by his side during his adventures.

[PROFILE]

Marcus
Brody

Bumbling but extremely well-meaning, Marcus Brody is one of Indy's most loyal friends. A curator at the history museum that stores many of Dr Jones' discoveries, Marcus cares passionately about preserving ancient treasures. Despite his lack of physical fortitude and organisation, Brody is always prepared to accompany Indy on his adventures.

[PROFILE]

Sallah

Another of Indy's most-trusted friends and the finest digger in Egypt, Sallah looks out for Dr Jones when he's in Cairo, giving him a place to stay and the provisions he requires. Sallah is charming and has a great sense of humour. He is often on hand to help Indy get out of tricky situations.

[PROFILE]

Belloq

Frenchman Belloq is Indy's greatest archaeological rival. Unlike Dr Jones, Belloq is happy to bend and break the rules to ensure he gets rich from the treasures he discovers, often stealing them out of Indy's hands.

[PROFILE]

Toht

The behaviour of the Nazi torturer Toht is as sinister as his appearance. The uncompromising German is willing to use any means necessary to extract information from his enemies and is a loyal servant to Adolf Hitler.

[PROFILE]

Dietrich

Abrupt and determined, Dietrich is a considerable rival to Indy, Sallah and Marion. The Nazi colonel keeps Belloq in check when distraction get the better of him and relishe deploying the techniques of torturer Toht.

[PROFILE]

RAIDERS of the LOST ARK

Indiana Jones is searching for an ancient idol in the Peruvian jungles in South America when he enters a booby-trap-ridden, tarantula-infested underground temple. Indy cautiously avoids the many traps inside and amazingly manages to recover the golden idol. But Indy is abandoned and double crossed by two men he hired to help find the idol and has to make a run for it as the temple walls crash down around him

Indy uses his trusty whip to escape by the skin of his teeth. After almost being squashed between closing walls and a huge rolling boulder, he emerges from the temple where he's immediately surrounded by a group of weapon-wielding tribesmen.

INDIANA JONES

"Belloq," Indy grunts, looking up in disbelief as his long-term enemy and rival confronts him. The Frenchman stands over Indy with an evil grin and forces him to hand over the treasure.

Indy escapes from the clutches of the tribesmen by seaplane and is forced to return home to America empty-handed.

Whilst he is teaching at Marshall College, intelligence officers from the Army pay Indy a visit. The intelligence officers tell Indy that the Nazis have teams of archaeologists scattered all of the world looking for many religious artefacts and that there is a German archaeological dig taking place in the desert outside Cairo, Egypt.

Indy works out that the Nazis have discovered the city of Tanis that is believed to be the resting place of the Ark of the Covenant. The Ark contains the Ten Commandments and enough power to wipe out entire armies.

Dr Jones' friend and colleague, Marcus Brody, tells him that Army Intelligence wants him to get hold of the Ark before the Nazis. Without hesitation, Indy swaps his suit and bow-tie for his famous leather jacket and hat as he prepares for another adventure.

Indy knows his former friend, Dr Abner Ravenwood, has a vast knowledge of the Ark and owns the headpiece of the Staff of Ra, which could guide him to the Ark's resting place. Indy takes a flight to Nepal to see his ex-girlfriend Marion, Ravenwood's daughter. Indy tracks Marion to a local bar where she's working but his old flame is far from happy when he turns up out of the blue. Indy asks for the headpiece, but Marion tells him to return the following day.

Moments after he leaves the Nazis arrive, also in search of the medallion, and they're not prepared to take "no" for an answer.

"What do you want?" Marion asks. "The same thing Dr Jones wanted," replies Toht, a Nazi torturer, before threatening Marion with a red-hot poker from the fire! In the nick of time, Indy returns to the bar to rescue Marion.

During the fight Toht attempts to grab the medallion from the floor. But it becomes red-hot and Toht screams and recoils in pain as he drops it. An imprint of the medallion is burned into his palm.

Indy and Marion leave the bar with the medallion and travel to Cairo. They meet up with Indy's trusty friend, Sallah. Indy isn't surprised to learn of the Nazi presence in Cairo and that his rival Belloq is helping them.

The Nazis track down Indy and
Marion and pursue them through
the city's streets and markets.
Indy fights off local swordsmen
and Nazi allies. Marion hides in a
basket but the Nazis find her and
bundle the basket into the back
of a truck carrying explosives to
the site of the dig.

Indy fires his revolver at the
truck, not realising Marion is
on board, causing the vehicle to
crash and explode. Indy believes
Marion has been killed and
drowns his sorrows in a local bar.
In the bar is Belloq who boasts
that he and the Nazis are close to
finding the Ark of the Covenant.
Using the image of the medallion
burned onto Toht's hand, the
Nazis - under an officer called
Dietrich - are trying to find the
resting place of the Ark.

Indy realises they are digging a mile away from the correct location as both sides of the medallion are needed to work out the ark's resting place. Accompanied by Sallah, he sneaks into the Nazi camp and uses both sides of the medallion to find the correct location.

Whilst walking around the camp with Sallah, Indy finds Marion tied up in a tent. "Marion, I thought you were dead!" he whispers with a huge smile on his face.

Marion is delighted to see Indy but is angry when he refuses to free her. Indy knows he cannot risk being seen by the Nazis.

Later that evening Indy, Sallah, and their team of diggers travel to the real location of the Ark. After digging all night, they finally discover a concealed entrance. Indy grabs a fire torch and drops it into the well to reveal why the floor appears to be moving. "Snakes, why did it have to be snakes," Indy groans. Hundreds of the deadly reptiles he hates are writhing around the bottom of the well.

I HATE SNAKES

Sallah lowers Indy down and Indy sprays the snakes with petrol. He sets them alight as he searches for the Ark.

Meanwhile Marion is untied by Belloq and attempts to escape using a knife she has concealed. But she is again confronted by the evil Toht, who is determined to extract information from her about the Ark.

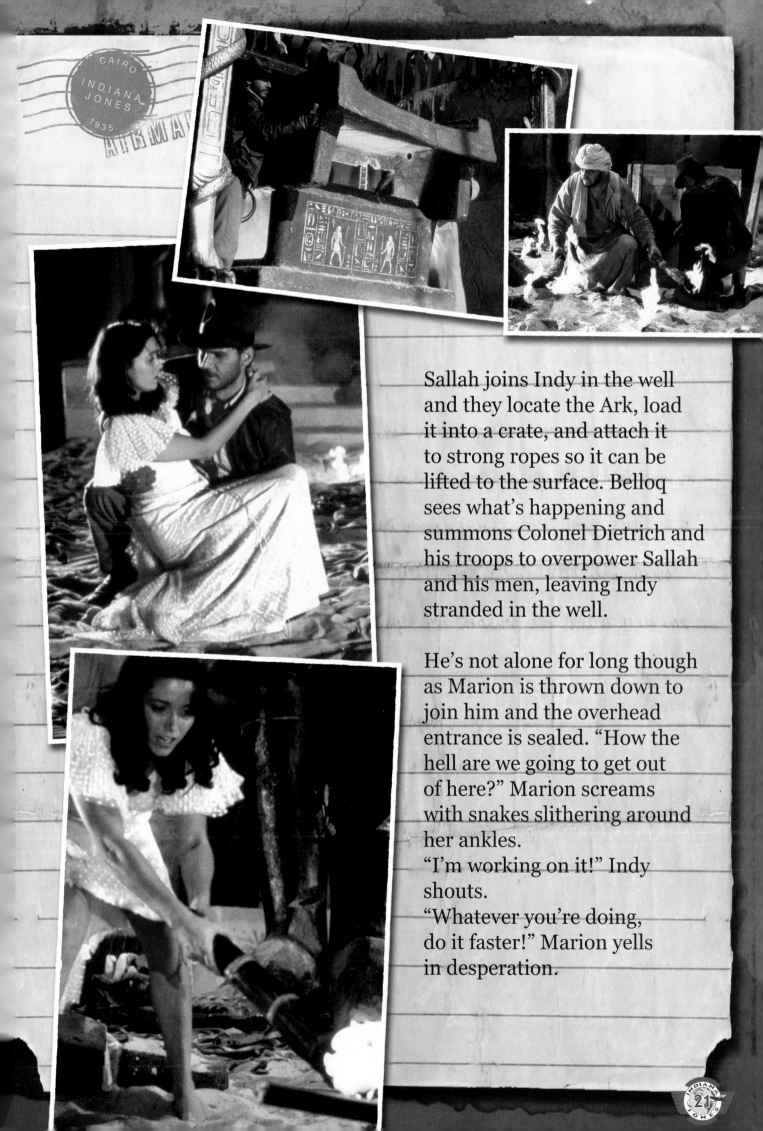

Sallah joins Indy in the well and they locate the Ark, load it into a crate, and attach it to strong ropes so it can be lifted to the surface. Belloq sees what's happening and summons Colonel Dietrich and his troops to overpower Sallah and his men, leaving Indy stranded in the well.

He's not alone for long though as Marion is thrown down to join him and the overhead entrance is sealed. "How the hell are we going to get out of here?" Marion screams with snakes slithering around her ankles.
"I'm working on it!" Indy shouts.
"Whatever you're doing, do it faster!" Marion yells in desperation.

After battling the snakes with fire from hand torches Indy discovers another exit. He and Marion make their way back to the surface and find a German plane. After a fierce battle with several soldiers the plane explodes and sets fire to much of the nearby camp.

Sallah informs Indy the Ark is now on a truck bound for Cairo. Indy pursues the Nazis on horseback, then fights them on moving vehicles travelling at breakneck speeds before escaping in the truck containing the Ark.

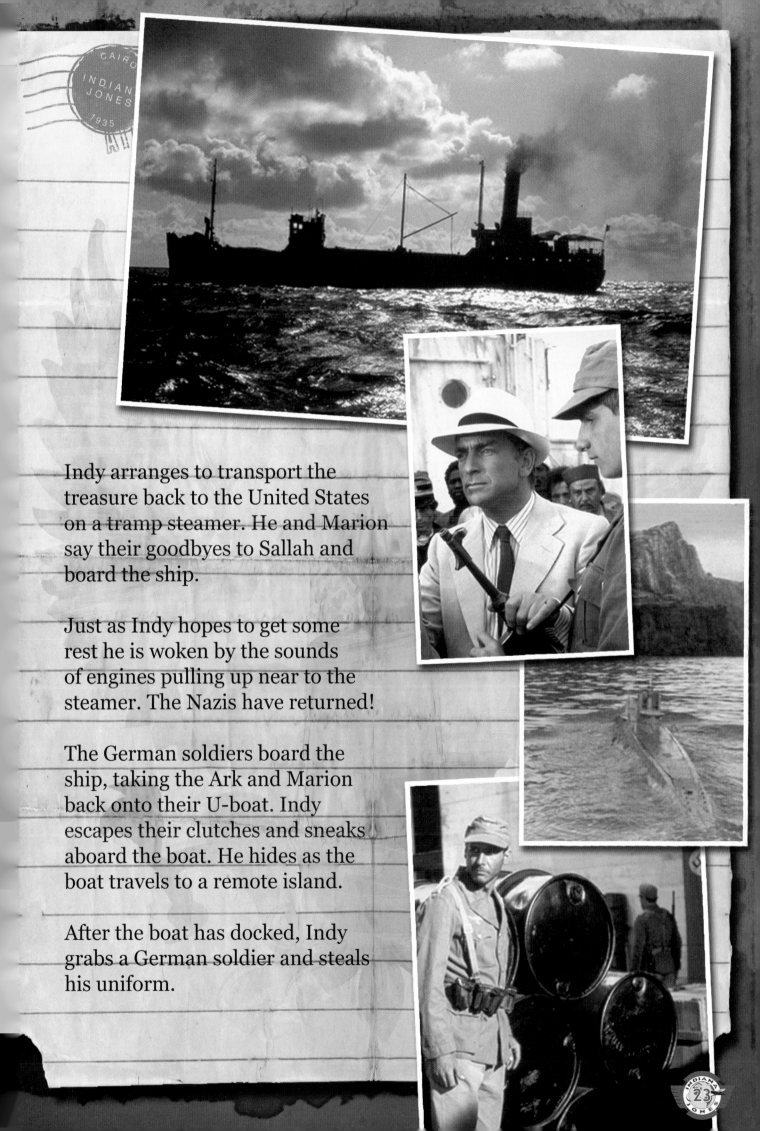

Indy arranges to transport the treasure back to the United States on a tramp steamer. He and Marion say their goodbyes to Sallah and board the ship.

Just as Indy hopes to get some rest he is woken by the sounds of engines pulling up near to the steamer. The Nazis have returned!

The German soldiers board the ship, taking the Ark and Marion back onto their U-boat. Indy escapes their clutches and sneaks aboard the boat. He hides as the boat travels to a remote island.

After the boat has docked, Indy grabs a German soldier and steals his uniform.

An alter is prepared for a secret ritual that will reveal the contents of the Ark. On his way to the ritual, Indy attempts to ambush Belloq, Dietrich and the soldiers but, greatly outnumbered, he is taken prisoner.

Tied to a wooden stake with Marion, Indy looks on in desperation as Belloq begins the ceremony. Two soldiers remove the lid from the Ark and ghostly apparitions emerge. A shaft of blinding light rises into the sky. Indy senses the Ark's power. "Don't look at it, no matter what happens!" he shouts to Marion, as he closes his eyes tightly.

Belloq is mesmerised by the light. "It's beautiful!" he shouts. Intense jets of flame shoot out of the Ark, killing a crowd of soldiers. Ghostly faces appear to turn into skeletons as they stare into the eyes of Belloq, Dietrich and Toht.

Belloq is engulfed in a huge fireball and the two Nazi officers melt into pools of slime as their skin and flesh melt away.

Another huge shaft of fire from the Ark shoots high into the sky, drops back down and seals the lid. Indy and Marion manage to untie themselves and escape.

Back in America, Indy begrudgingly hands the Ark over to government officials.
"You've done your country a great service Doctor Jones," they tell him, explaining the Ark will not be going on display in a museum.

Indy is left frustrated. "Fools, bureaucratic fools!" he fumes, "They don't know they've got there!"
"Well I know what I've got here." Marion replies, smiling at Indy as the pair walk off arm in arm.

The Ark is sealed in a chest and hidden in a secure US Government warehouse. Indy cannot help but think about the extreme powers the Ark contains but he is glad to be safe following one of his most exciting adventures.

Indiana Jones

After each of the four adventures see how much you can remember by taking the quizzes...

1. In which country is Marion running a bar?
Answer:

2. Which university does Indy lecture at?
Answer:

3. What nationality is Indy's archaeological rival Belloq?
Answer:

4. In which Egyptian city is the Ark believed to be located?
Answer:

5. Which reptile do we find out that Indy hates?
Answer:

6. Where does Marion hide in the Egyptian market place when she is being pursued by the Nazis?
Answer:

7. What is the name of the evil Nazi torturer who burns his hand on the medallion?
Answer:

8. What is the full name of the Ark that Indy is searching for?
Answer:

9. What is the name of Marion's father?
Answer:

10. What is the name of Nazi colonel who tries to foil Indy?
Answer:

11. What is the name of Indy's Egyptian friend who helps him defeat the Nazis?
Answer:

12. Other than Indy, who takes a shine to Marion, Dietrich and Belloq?
Answer:

13. When the bright lights shoot out of the Ark what's Indy's advice to Marion?
Answer:

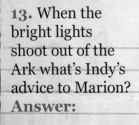

14. What type of building is the Ark eventually stored in once Indy delivers it to the US Government?
Answer:

SPOT THE DIFFERENCE

Study these two pictures from *Raiders of the Lost Ark*. There are five differences. Are you as eagle-eyed as Indy and can you spot them all?

WHO AM I?

Use the powers of deduction that Indy is famed for and decipher each of the following clues to work out the character to which they refer.

1. This young chap may not be tall, but his heart and spirit for the battle are huge. One of Indy's most loyal friends.

Answer: . . . .

2. A German torturer caught red-handed by Indy and Marion.

Answer: . . . .

3. Rich collector obsessed with the Holy Grail and eternal youth. Money doesn't buy him any class, though.

Answer: . . . .

4. The best digger in Egypt and an extremely hospitable host to Dr Jones.

Answer: . . . .

5. Glamorous American singer who would rather live the life of luxury then get her hands dirty going on further adventures with Indiana.

Answer: . . . .

6. A strong-willed Ukrainian doctor, determined to gain knowledge and power.

Answer: . . . .

7. This Englishman temporarily loses his marbles after finding the famous crystal skull.

Answer: . . . .

8. Indy's argumentative love interest whilst he's searching for the Ark of the Covenant and the crystal skull.

Answer: . . . .

9. Money-obsessed double agent who turns against Indy and ends up with a broken nose.

Answer: . . . .

10. The son Indy never realised he had, although they don't share the same surname.

Answer: . . . .

RAIDERS OF THE LOST ARK
WORD SEARCH

Try to find the words listed below in this special *Raiders of the Lost Ark* word search. The words can be written horizontally, vertically, backwards and diagonally in both directions.

A	W	U	K	S	L	C	C	P	H	R	Y
V	J	F	Y	E	S	A	I	O	S	W	Q
O	O	U	H	K	E	D	C	Q	K	O	Y
P	O	I	N	A	G	C	X	D	L	T	Y
Q	L	K	J	N	G	F	D	L	A	E	H
R	T	K	J	S	P	U	E	N	D	M	A
S	E	T	X	K	N	B	G	H	Y	U	L
A	Q	S	W	E	X	Z	Z	J	B	F	L
O	R	H	U	D	E	S	B	M	V	C	A
J	N	K	B	D	F	O	I	Y	U	I	S
Z	A	L	G	Y	B	N	X	Z	Q	N	G
E	T	N	L	M	M	D	F	S	A	C	U
P	F	K	N	T	S	S	R	R	N	N	O
V	B	A	G	N	A	T	A	K	S	D	E
L	K	G	N	V	I	R	P	W	Q	N	C
B	N	U	O	S	D	F	H	J	C	Q	X
S	U	V	J	N	L	A	P	E	N	T	U
P	T	D	V	G	H	S	D	K	N	O	O
B	I	K	J	D	C	O	P	S	D	W	Q
H	G	Y	I	D	O	A	A	E	X	V	E
T	D	I	E	T	R	I	C	H	E	F	A
S	K	L	C	A	A	U	O	O	O	D	J

- ☐ ARK
- ☐ NEPAL
- ☐ DIETRICH
- ☐ SALLAH
- ☐ BELLOQ
- ☐ SNAKES
- ☐ KATANGA
- ☐ NAZIS

WHO SAID WHAT?

Draw a line to link the correct character to the famous quote or catchphrase they have used during one of the films...

Short
Round

Indiana
Jones

Sallah

Dr Irina
Spalko

"I intuit things. I know them before anyone else, and what I do not know, I learn."

Harold
'Ox'Oxley

"Don't call me Junior!"

"If you listen to me, you'll live longer"

"I can't go to Pankot, I'm a singer!"

"To lay their just hands on that Golden Key that ope's the Palace of Eternity."

"Indy, why does the floor move?"

"Well what can I say Jonesy? I'm a capitalist, and they pay."

"Fortune and glory kid, fortune and glory!"

"The healing power of the Grail is the only thing that can save your father now."

George
'Mac' McHale

"Indiana Jones. Are you still leaving a trail of human wreckage behind you everywhere you go?"

Willie
Scott

Walter
Donovan

Marion
Ravenwood

Indiana
Jones

31

10 QUESTIONS
ABOUT INDIANA JONES

Check how much you know about adventurer Indiana Jones. Pick one of the three answers for each question.

1. Which animal does Indy have a fear of?

a) Elephants ☐
b) Crocodiles ☐
c) Snakes ☐

2. At which college does Doctor Jones teach?

a) Yale ☐
b) Washington ☐
c) Marshall ☐

3. Name the French archaeologist who is one of Indy's main rivals.

a) Dr Irina Spalko ☐
b) Belloq ☐
c) Sallah ☐

4. In which year did Indy go in search of the Ark of the Covenant?

a) 1937 ☐
b) 1963 ☐
c) 1936 ☐

5. Which country does Indy visit to find Marion working in a bar?

a) Egypt ☐
b) Turkey ☐
c) Nepal ☐

6. What is the name of the Chinese nightclub where Indy first meets Willie Scott?

a) Club Obi-Wan ☐
b) Club One-Okay ☐
c) The One Club ☐

7. Indy is forced to drink the blood of which god whilst battling the Thuggee cult in Pankot?

a) Thugar ☐
b) Kali ☐
c) Mola Ram ☐

8. In which German city does Indy meet Nazi leader Adolf Hitler whilst reclaiming his father's Holy Grail diary?

a) Munich ☐
b) Hamburg ☐
c) Berlin ☐

9. Who shoots Indy's father, Professor Henry Jones Senior?

a) Walter Donovan ☐
b) Marcus Brody ☐
c) Dietrich ☐

10. Who tells Indy that Mutt Williams is his son?

a) Marion Ravenwood ☐
b) Harold Oxley ☐
c) Dr Irina Spalko ☐

INDIANA JONES 1935 AIRMAIL

TEMPLE OF DOOM

Willie
Scott

[PROFILE]

A glamorous American singer, Willie Scott is one of the most highly-strung women Indy has ever met. Willie hates getting her hands dirty and roughing it in the jungle. She likes being pampered and living in the lap of luxury in China. Despite finding Indy irritating and holding him responsible for putting her in danger, Miss Scott holds a torch for Doctor Jones.

Short
Round

Indy's young Chinese friend is worth his weight in gold during their adventures. Intelligent and cheeky, Shorty knows no fear and despite his small frame has the courage and tenacity to take on much larger enemies. Has saved Indy's bacon on more than one occasion.

[PROFILE]

Mola
Ram

Mola Ram is the evil high priest of the ancient and wicked Thuggee cult. Using the power of the Sankara stones Mola Ram has the frightening ability to pull out people's still-beating hearts. His commitment to the Thuggee god, Kali, and his obsession with making human sacrifices makes him one of Indy's toughest adversaries.

[PROFILE]

Maharajah
of Pankot

The Maharajah of Pankot, this Highness Zalim Singh, is a young but extremely powerful boy that sits on the Palace throne. His loyal advisor is Pankot's Prime Minister, Chattar Lal. The Maharajah is under some sort of a trance until Indy and Shorty take on the evil Thuggees.

[PROFILE]

INDIANA JONES ™
and the
TEMPLE OF DOOM

A year before tracking down the Ark of the Covenant, Indy is in Shanghai, China, drinking in a cocktail bar called Obi-Wan. Dressed in a white tuxedo, Indy meets the members of a Chinese organised crime group and their boss, Lao Che.

Performing at the bar is a beautiful American singer called Willie Scott. Willie sits next to Indy as Lao and his men are introduced.

Lao has agreed to pay Indy with a huge diamond in return for a rare Chinese artefact he has found, but when it comes to the crunch, Lao refuses to pay, angering Doctor Jones.

One of the men points a gun at Indy, demanding he hand over the artefact. Indy quickly holds a knife against the singer, putting himself in a better bargaining position. "The diamond Lao," Indy demands, "give me the diamond!"
As the exchange is made, Lao is clearly delighted with his purchase.

"Inside are the remains of Nurhachi, the first Emperor of the Manchu dynasty," he explains with a sinister smile.

Indy sips his drink to celebrate the deal then realises he's been poisoned by Lao! Lao and his men erupt in fits of laughter and demand the diamond back in return for an antidote.

An old friend of Indy's, Wu Hun, who is dressed as a waiter, tries to assist, but is shot by one of Lao's men.

"Don't be sad Doctor Jones, you will soon be joining him," Lao says with a chuckle.

More shots are fired and the diamond and antidote roll across the floor of the bar as Indy and Willie desperately try to grab them. After Willie manages to get the antidote, Indy grabs her and the pair jump through a window and land in the back of the car being driven by another of Indy's trusted friends, Short Round.

"How the hell does a kid drive a car?" Willie screams as Short Round dodges in and out of the busy Shanghai roads, to the airport.

SHANGHAI CHINA

They board a freight plane – but it belongs to Lao - and his pilots dump the craft's fuel and parachute out of it while Indy, Willy and Short Round sleep.

Realizing the plane will soon crash, Indy grabs the controls and discovers the fuel is depleted. With no chance of landing safely, Indy instructs Shorty to inflate a life raft. The three jump out of the plane and inside the raft land safely on the snow-covered mountains as the plane crashes into rocks and explodes.

The raft slides out of control, skims off the edge of a mountain, down a sheer drop and into fierce rapids below. As the river slows they can finally relax.

"Where are we anyway?"
Willie asks.
"India," Indy replies, noticing a man in traditional Indian clothing.

The old man guides them to a nearby village, called Mayapore, where the desperate inhabitants beg for help. The old man says he will provide them with a guide to Delhi but they must stop off at Pankot Palace on the way to collect a Sankara stone that has been stolen from the village.

The man tells Indy that after the stone was taken, water wells dried up and animals turned into dust. One night there was a fire in the fields and the men went to fight it. When they returned all of the village's children had disappeared.

Later that evening a boy limps into the village and, exhausted, falls into Indy's arms. "Sankara, Sankara," he struggles to say before collapsing. He hands Indy a cloth patchwork with an image of the Sankara stone.

Indy, Willie and Shorty are provided with guides and elephants for the journey to Pankot. At the Palace gates, the trio are greeted by Prime Minister, Chattar Lal. He gives them rooms for the night and invites them to dinner with the Maharajah of Pankot, his Highness Zalim Singh.

The Maharajah is a child. "That's the Maharajah?" Willie groans, "A kid?" "Maybe he likes older women?" Shorty jokes.

The food provided doesn't match the luxurious surroundings and Willie is repulsed by the local delicacies of snakes, beetles and chilled monkey brains.

Indy discusses the Thuggee cult and what the villagers have told him with the Prime Minister. Chatter Lal tries to reassure Indy that the stories are just folklore and that the Thuggee cult has been dead for over a century.

Indy isn't convinced. That night a member of the palace staff attacks Indy in his room and tries to strangle him with a wire. Indy fights the man off with the help of Shorty and his whip.

Indy and Shortly discover a secret passageway leading to an underground world beneath the palace. But the pair find themselves in serious trouble when Shorty accidentally activates a booby trap, imprisoning them in a small room.

As spike-covered walls start to cave in on them they shout to Willie for help. Scared stiff and repulsed by the bugs she has to walk over, Willie eventually plucks up enough courage to reach the insect-covered handle that stops the walls and spikes just in time.

Further down the passageway they hear the sound of gongs and men chanting – and witness the Thuggee ceremony during which a man is sacrificed to the Thuggee god, Kali.

The evil Mola Ram, high priest of the Thuggees, rips out the man's still-beating heart. Amazingly, the man survives and is strapped inside a metal cage and plunged into a fiery pool of lava. The empty cage is lifted back to the surface.

The stone stolen from the village, plus two similar stones, are spotted inside a rock skull, and all three of the Sankara stones light up. Indy clambers across the rocks and, using his trusty whip, swings down to the stones. He grabs the village's stone and stashes it in his knapsack.

As Indy is distracted by the screams and cries of the thousands of children being forced to dig for the last Sankara stones in the catacombs below the palace, Willie and Short are captured by the evil army. Indy is also taken prisoner.

In jail, two children explain to Indy about the Thuggees and Kali, who people are forced to worship after taking one sip of his blood.

Indy is forced to drink the blood and is brainwashed into believing in Kali and follows the evil direction of the high priest of the Thuggee cult, the Mola Ram.

Completely under the spell of Kali, Indy unknowingly takes an active part in the next sacrificial ceremony as Willie is offered to the Thuggee god.

As the entranced Indy walks over to Willie to take the next steps of the ritual, Shorty smashes through his chains and runs towards the ceremony. He attacks the soldiers with a flaming torch and strikes the dazed Indy.

Indy snaps out of the trance and stops the guards from killing Shorty. They battle their enemies and save Willie from the burning lava with just inches to spare.

Mola Ram escapes down a hidden trapdoor, rolling away to safety with an evil cackle, but the Prime Minister is stopped in his tracks as he tries to prevent Indy from saving Willie.

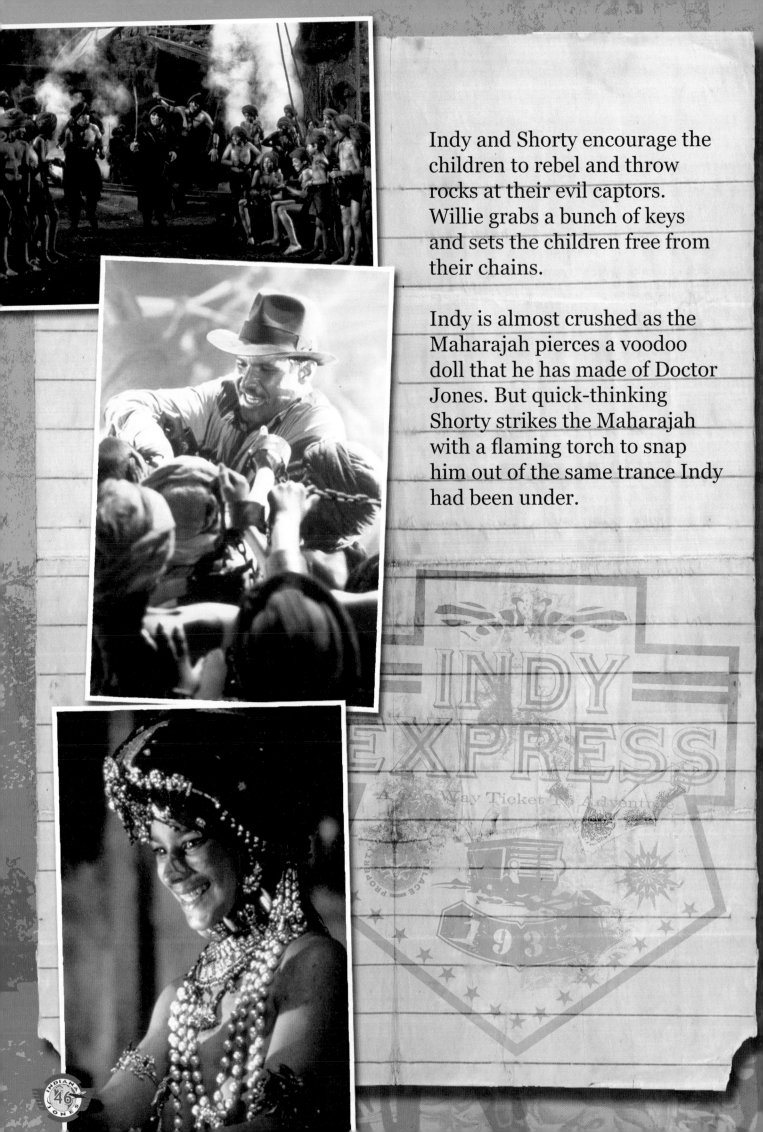

Indy and Shorty encourage the children to rebel and throw rocks at their evil captors. Willie grabs a bunch of keys and sets the children free from their chains.

Indy is almost crushed as the Maharajah pierces a voodoo doll that he has made of Doctor Jones. But quick-thinking Shorty strikes the Maharajah with a flaming torch to snap him out of the same trance Indy had been under.

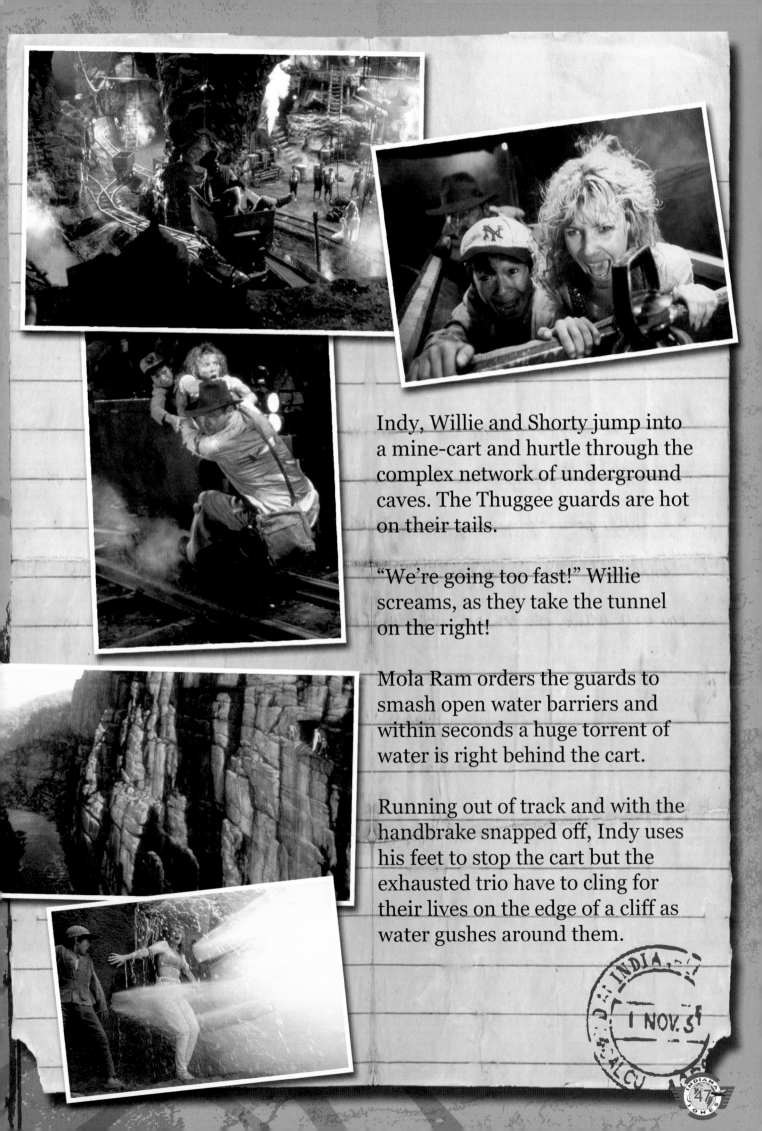

Indy, Willie and Shorty jump into a mine-cart and hurtle through the complex network of underground caves. The Thuggee guards are hot on their tails.

"We're going too fast!" Willie screams, as they take the tunnel on the right!

Mola Ram orders the guards to smash open water barriers and within seconds a huge torrent of water is right behind the cart.

Running out of track and with the handbrake snapped off, Indy uses his feet to stop the cart but the exhausted trio have to cling for their lives on the edge of a cliff as water gushes around them.

Shorty and Willie make it to a rickety rope bridge hanging over crocodile-infested waters. But as they cross to the other side Mola Ram greets them. Indy runs across the bridge but is trapped with guards behind him and the Mola Ram and Thuggees in front.

"Hang on, we're going for a ride!" says Indy, as he cuts through the bridge with a sword. Many Thuggees fall to their death as Indy and Mola Ram battle and hang on to what's left of the dangling bridge.

Indy chants the ancient words that make the magic stones in his knapsack glow. They burn through the bag and all but one fall into the river. Mola Ram grabs it, but it burns his hand and he loses his grip, falling into the depths where he is torn to shreds by the crocodiles.

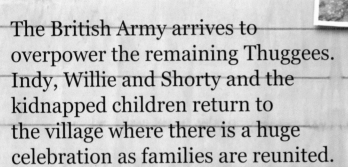

The British Army arrives to overpower the remaining Thuggees. Indy, Willie and Shorty and the kidnapped children return to the village where there is a huge celebration as families are reunited.

Indy returns the stone to its rightful resting place, relieved and satisfied as another adventure is completed with a happy ending.

INDIANA JONES

IT'S NOT THE YEARS

SINCE 1935

IT'S THE MILEAGE

FORTUNE & GLORY

INDIANA JONES

QUIZ 2 : Temple Of Doom

Well done! You managed to get past the first obstacle. Now you have to navigate yourself through the next set of questions.

1. What is the name of the Chinese cocktail bar where Willie Scott was singing?
Answer:

2. How does Shorty rescue Indy and Willie as they attempt to escape the Obi-Wan club?
Answer:

3. Which village are Indy and his friends led to following the plane crash?
Answer:

4. Whose remains did Indy recover for Lao?
Answer:

5. What is the name of Pankot's Prime Minister?
Answer:

6. In return for the remains he has retrieved for Lao, what is Indy expecting as payment?
Answer:

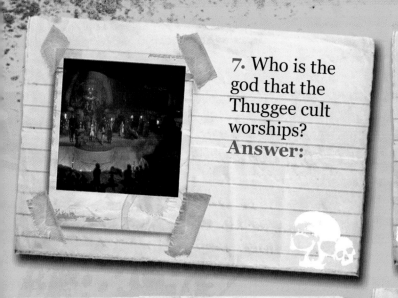

7. Who is the god that the Thuggee cult worships?
Answer:

8. When they are on the rail cart, which track do the adventurers take, the left or right?
Answer:

9. On which kind of animal do Indy, Willie and Shorty ride to the Pankot Palace?
Answer:

10. What is the name of the Maharajah?
Answer:

11. After being taken to the village which city does Indy want to reach?
Answer:

12. In which country does the plane carrying Indy and his friends crash?
Answer:

13. Which part of a monkey is served up for dinner at the Pankot Palace?
Answer:

14. What are the stones kept in the underground caves of Pankot called?
Answer:

SPOT THE DIFFERENCE

Study these two pictures from *Temple of Doom*. There are five differences, can you be as eagle-eyed as Indy and spot them all?

TEMPLE OF DOOM WORD SEARCH

Try to find the words listed below in this special *Temple of Doom* word search. The words can be written horizontally, vertically, backwards and diagonally in both directions.

A	W	U	K	S	L	C	C	P	H	R	Y
V	J	W	Y	M	A	R	A	L	O	M	Q
O	O	U	H	B	E	D	C	Q	K	I	Y
S	O	I	S	O	T	C	X	D	X	T	Y
E	L	K	J	R	G	F	D	A	A	E	H
E	W	I	L	L	I	E	S	C	O	T	T
G	E	T	X	K	N	B	G	H	Y	U	O
G	Q	S	W	E	X	Z	Z	J	M	F	X
U	A	H	U	D	E	S	B	A	V	C	L
H	N	O	B	D	F	O	H	Y	U	I	E
T	A	R	G	Y	B	A	X	Z	Q	N	G
E	T	T	L	M	R	D	F	S	A	C	K
P	F	Y	N	A	S	S	R	R	N	A	O
V	B	A	J	A	A	N	A	L	L	D	E
L	A	H	N	V	I	R	P	I	Q	N	C
Z	A	R	O	S	D	F	A	J	C	Q	X
T	U	V	A	N	L	J	P	C	N	T	U
O	T	D	V	K	H	S	D	P	N	O	O
K	I	K	J	D	N	O	P	S	D	W	Q
N	G	A	I	O	O	A	A	E	X	V	E
A	Z	A	L	S	R	I	S	K	E	F	A
P	K	L	C	A	A	U	O	O	O	D	J

- ☐ SHORTY
- ☐ SANKARA
- ☐ MOLA RAM
- ☐ KALI
- ☐ WILLIE SCOTT
- ☐ PANKOT
- ☐ MAHARAJAH
- ☐ THUGGEES

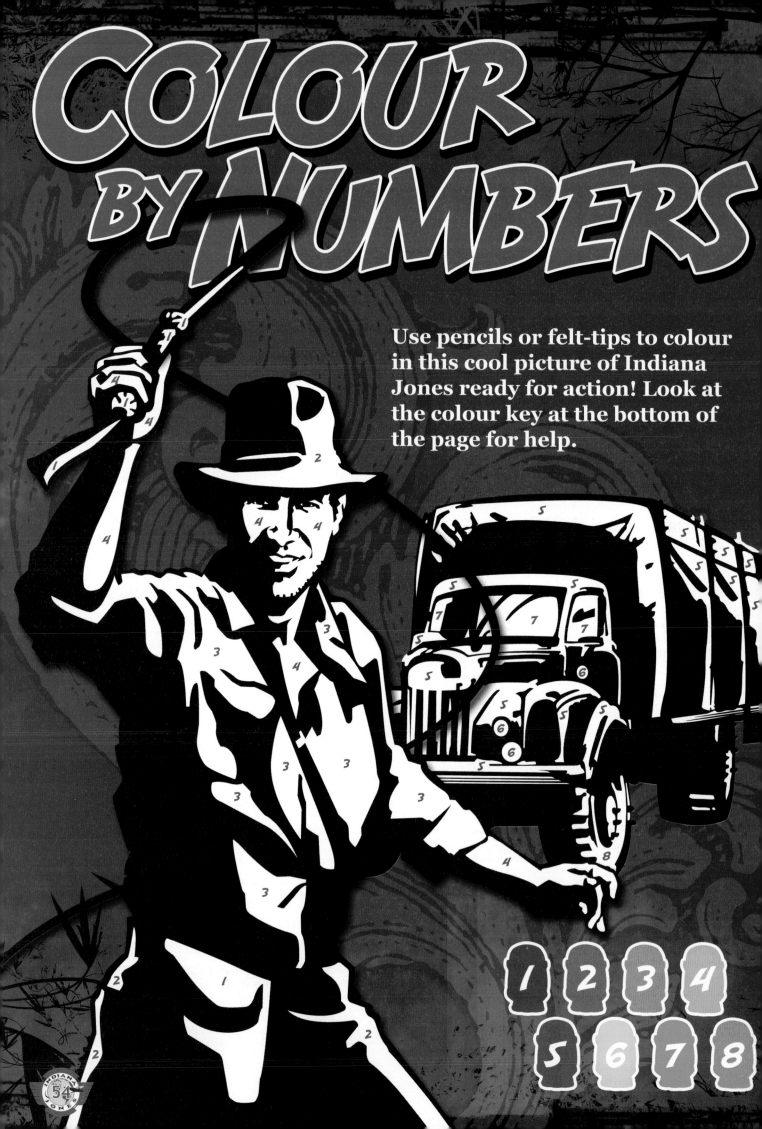

10 QUESTIONS
ABOUT THE VILLAINS

How much can you remember about the enemies Indy and has friends have had to face over the years? Pick one of the three options for each of the questions.

1. Which leader of the Thuggee cult battled Indy on the remains of a rickety bridge?

a) Sallah ☐
b) Mola Ram ☐
c) Dietrich ☐

2. Who shoots Doctor Jones' friend Wu Hun and refuses to pay Indy the diamond he owes him?

a) Short Round ☐
b) Obi-Wan ☐
c) Lao Che ☐

3. What is the name of the Prime Minister of Pankot?

a) Chattar Lal ☐
b) Mola Ram ☐
c) Lao Che ☐

4. Which Russian General has two fierce fights with Indy during their quest to find the city of gold?

a) Belloq ☐
b) Antonin Dovchenko ☐
c) Mutski Williamochev ☐

5. Which of Indy's rivals takes a shine to Marion during his quest to find the Ark of the Covenant?

a) Dietrich ☐
b) Antonin Dovchenko ☐
c) Belloq ☐

6. What is the name of the Russian KGB agent who boasts of "receiving the order of Lenin on three separate occasions?"

a) Dr Ireen Palsko ☐
b) Dr Elana Spalchev ☐
c) Dr Irina Spalko ☐

7. Dr Elsa Schneider tricks Indy into believing that she is on his side, but with which set of soldiers is she really siding with?

a) The Russians ☐
b) The Nazis ☐
c) The Thuggee Cult ☐

8. Whose body crumbles to dust after taking a swig of water from the wrong cup whilst searching for the Holy Grail?

a) Marcus Brody ☐
b) Dietrich ☐
c) Walter Donovan ☐

9. Which frightening foe has the power to rip out people's still-beating hearts?

a) Rola Jam ☐
b) Mola Ram ☐
c) Jolo Rum ☐

10. What is the name of the evil Nazi interrogator who confronts Marion in Nepal?

a) Toht ☐
b) Toast ☐
c) Antonin Dovchenko ☐

Worldwide Adventure

INDIANA JONES

Since 1935

FORTUNE AND GLORY

57

The Third Instalment...

THE LAST CRUSADE

Walter
Donovan

Walter Donovan is a super-rich collector of antiques and ancient artefacts. He is determined to find the Holy Grail and is obsessed with regaining his youth and becoming immortal. This obsession leads to him making some questionable decisions as he aligns himself with evil forces to get what he wants.

[PROFILE]

Marcus
Brody

Marcus is very much involved in this adventure. Thrown in at the deep end by Indy, he is often targeted as a weak point and finds himself in serious danger on more than one occasion.

[PROFILE]

Dr Elsa
Schneider

[PROFILE]

Dr Schneider is an extremely beautiful and intelligent woman, whose knowledge of history and mythology appear to be a match for Indy. Elsa understands the power of the Holy Grail even though her motives are often more evil than good. Eventually her quest for the Grail leads her to question these motives, but is it too late to save her soul?

Dr Henry
Jones Senior

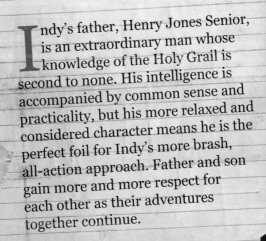

[PROFILE]

Indy's father, Henry Jones Senior, is an extraordinary man whose knowledge of the Holy Grail is second to none. His intelligence is accompanied by common sense and practicality, but his more relaxed and considered character means he is the perfect foil for Indy's more brash, all-action approach. Father and son gain more and more respect for each other as their adventures together continue.

Sallah

[PROFILE]

Indy's loyal friend is again at his side during this adventure, providing vehicles, provisions and a much-needed ally against the Nazis.

INDIANA JONES
and the
LAST CRUSADE

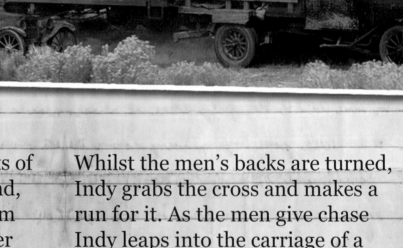

The year is 1912. In the deserts of Utah young Indy and his friend, Herman, wander off away from their group of Scouts and enter a rocky cave.

They discover that a group of men digging through the cave walls have found a golden cross. Crouching behind a rock, Indy whispers to Herman "It's the Cross of Coronado. It is an artefact and it belongs in a museum."

Whilst the men's backs are turned, Indy grabs the cross and makes a run for it. As the men give chase Indy leaps into the carriage of a train steaming along the tracks.

The men also jump aboard and pursue him from carriage to carriage. Indy flees from their clutches and runs all the way home, bursting into his father's office shouting about the cross. His busy father takes little notice of his son's latest discovery.

Herman then arrives with the sheriff, who tells Indy to give the cross back to its rightful owner. The men who dug it up enter the house and a man smartly dressed in a white suit waits outside for the cross.

"You lost today kid," says the leader. "But it doesn't mean you have to like it," he adds giving Indy his fedora - a gift Indy will treasure and wear during later adventures.

Years later, in 1938, Indy is on a fishing boat off the Portuguese coast and fighting the man in the white suit for the possession of the same golden cross.

"This is the second time I've had to reclaim my property from you!" the man shouts as he grabs the cross from Indy's bag.

"That cross belongs in a museum!" Indy says for a second time, jumping overboard and onto a life raft as the ship explodes.

Indy returns to New York to lecture at Barnett College where he meets up with his old friend Marcus Brody. Marcus puts the cross on display in his museum.

Indy receives an intriguing package postmarked Venice, Italy. As students and staff pester him, Indy clambers out of his office window and outside is invited to a meeting with multi-millionaire, Walter Donovan. Donovan explains he has discovered an amazing stone tablet that he shows to Indy.

He asks Indy to translate the inscription that speaks of the Holy Grail, the chalice used by Christ during the Last Supper and the cup that caught his blood at the crucifixion. The stone is the first of three hidden markers that reveal the location of the Holy Grail.

"I've heard this bedtime story before," says Indy, who believes the Holy Grail is nothing more than a myth.

"Eternal life, Doctor Jones!" Donovan replies. "The gift of youth to whoever drinks from the Grail. Now that's a bedtime story I'd like to wake up to."

Donovan reveals that an expert he hired to help locate the Grail has gone missing. To Indy's horror Donovan reveals the missing person is Indy's father, Professor Henry Jones Senior, a keen researcher of the Holy Grail.

Indy and Marcus find that the home of Dr Jones Sr has been trashed and searched from top to bottom. Concerned for his father, Indy remembers the package from Venice and opens it to find his father's treasured Grail diary, which contains his research of the legend.

"What's the old fool got himself into now?" asks Marcus.
"I don't know," says Indy.
"But whatever is it, he's in over his head."
"Call Donovan, tell him I'll take his ticket to Venice now," says Indy.

The pair are met in Venice by Dr Elsa Schneider who takes them to a library where Indy uses the Grail diary to work out a cryptic puzzle that involves Roman numerals that appear on a huge stained glass window in the library, which used to be a church.

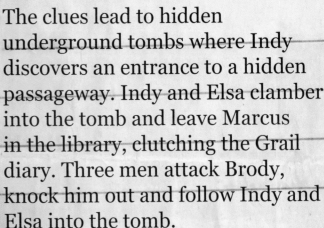

The clues lead to hidden underground tombs where Indy discovers an entrance to a hidden passageway. Indy and Elsa clamber into the tomb and leave Marcus in the library, clutching the Grail diary. Three men attack Brody, knock him out and follow Indy and Elsa into the tomb.

Behind an unstable stone wall Indy finds a rat-infested, petroleum covered walkway. This is what they've been looking for, the second marker. Another tablet gives further information that will lead them to the Holy Grail.

Indy's delight is short-lived as he hears the spark of a match and the roar of flames. Thousands of rats scurry towards them as a massive ball of fire ignites the oil. The pair hide under the tomb to shelter themselves from the flames before making their escape.

Climbing back up to the street level through a manhole, Indy and Dr Schneider are chased by the men who lit the fire. They leap into a speedboat and are pursued along the waterways of Venice.

Indy overcomes one of the men and questions him to discover they are part of an ancient order called the Brotherhood of the Cruciform Sword, whose job it has been to protect the Grail for hundreds of years. The man tells Indy his father is being held at Brunwald Castle in Austria, on the German border.

Indy sends Marcus to Turkey to meet his old friend Sallah as he and Elsa drive to Austria to rescue his father. When they get to the castle, Indy sneaks past the butler then realises Brunwald is occupied by Adolf Hitler's Nazi soldiers. "Nazis, I hate these guys," Indy grimaces.

He smashes through the window of the room were his father is being held. His dad smashes a porcelain jug over Indy's head, not realising the intruder is his son!

"Junior!" he says, "What are you doing here?"
"Don't call me that!" Indy replies through gritted teeth.
He tells his father the tale of the second Grail marker and how he has found the castle.

INDIANA JONES
HAVE WHIP·WILL TRAVEL

65

Armed Nazi soldiers storm into the room. Indy and his father argue, as Doctor Jones Sr believes Indy has brought the Grail diary with him. Indy overpowers the soldiers as the Jones' escape to another room. They are met by a Nazi colonel who is holding a gun to Elsa's head.

Henry Sr warns him not to trust Elsa. "She's one of them!" he pleads. But, Indy, who has taken a shine to Elsa, ignores his father's advice and drops the weapon. Elsa admits she's a Nazi, and Indy immediately regrets his decision.

As Walter Donovan appears, Indy realises he is also siding with Hitler and the Nazis. Dr Schneider takes the diary from Indy's pocket but notices that Indy has removed the crucial pages that reveal the next clues for the location of the Grail.

Schneider guesses Indy has given the pages to Marcus Brody. Indy and his father are tied together as Schneider and Donovan begin their pursuit of Marcus. The doctors attempt to free themselves from the ropes using a cigarette lighter but inadvertently set fire to the room.

After a brief fight with more soldiers the pair escape the castle on a motorbike. When they reach a crossroads, Indy is determined to head to Turkey to save Marcus but his father insists they travel to Berlin as Donovan has the other pages of the diary.

Indy agrees with his father, knowing that without the diary it would be impossible to prevent the Nazis from gaining the Grail.

Indy arrives in Berlin and walks straight into a ceremony being held by Adolf Hitler where hundreds of books are being burned. Disguised as a Nazi solider, Indy sneaks up on Schneider and grabs the diary. As he makes his escape, Indy bumps into Hitler! Neither man speaks but Hitler grabs the diary from Indy, signs it and returns it!

Indiana Jones 1935 U.S. POSTAGE

PB METER

J070466

Indy and his father leave the German capital aboard a zeppelin airship but the Colonel tracks them down. Indy pretends to be a ticket collector and pushes the Colonel overboard before take-off.

The determined Nazi doesn't give up that easily and instructs the ship's pilots to turn it around mid-flight and head back to Berlin.

Indy drags his father below deck and into a plane attached to the bottom of the zeppelin.

They take off and after a fierce dogfight with several Nazi pilots, Indy successfully lands the plane. The pair steal a car and speed off.

A plane drops a bomb in front of the car, causing it to fall into a deep crater. The Joneses continue their escape on foot but end up stranded on a beach with a third plane overhead ready to attack.

As it makes its final descent, Henry Sr scares a flock of grounded birds that fly into the plane's engines and obscure the pilot's vision. The aircraft crashes into cliffs.

Meanwhile Donovan travels to the Republic of Hatay with the Colonel and Doctor Schneider and catches up with Marcus.

Indy and his father meet up with Sallah in Turkey, who reveals that the Nazis have taken Marcus prisoner and that they have the map needed to locate the Grail.

Indy, his father, and Sallah watch as Donovan and the Nazis approach the site of the Grail. A gunfight starts when the Nazis are ambushed by soldiers from the Brotherhood of the Cruciform Sword, who are determined to save the grail.

Indiana Jones

We do not follow maps to buried treasure, and I never, ever marks the spot

IN INDY
WE TRUST

Kathmandu
Kanpur
Berlin
Venice
Cairo

Fortune and Glory

Trusted since 1935

Indy then launches his own attack on horseback as his father and Marcus are taken prisoner inside a tank.

The tank carrying the Colonel, Marcus and Professor Jones crashes into the other vehicles as Indy battles to rescue his father and Marcus. Indy clambers onto the top of the tank and saves Marcus and his father just before the tank drives off a steep cliff.

The Colonel falls to his doom as the crushed tank rolls along the pit of the ravine.

Sallah, Marcus and Henry Sr think Indy has also perished in the fall. But as they begin to mourn his loss, Indy clambers over the top of the canyon.

Meanwhile, Donovan and Schneider have continued their quest for the Grail and discover 'The Canyon of the Crescent Moon', which leads them to the resting place of the holy chalice.

Indy, his father and their friends discover a huge temple entrance, carved into the rock face. They sneak in to find one of the soldiers attempting to walk through a cobwebbed passageway to the Grail's resting place. He fails when a flying sword slices off his head.

Indy and his friends are discovered and Donovan insists Indy walk through the passageway to retrieve the holy treasure. When he refuses, Donovan shoots Henry Sr in the stomach.

"The healing power of the grail is the only thing that can save your father now!" Donovan says.

Indy begins to nervously edge through the passageway. "The penitent man will pass, the penitent man will pass," Indy repeats to himself as he tries to work out what the clue, contained in his father's Grail diary, means.

"The penitent man kneels before God," Indy shouts, dropping to his knees and narrowly avoiding a protruding blade.

The next challenge is called 'Proceed in the footsteps of the word'. The floor is covered in lettered tiles and Indy is able to work out the next clue.

"The word of God," he says to himself before spelling out the name of God and safely crossing the unstable pathway.

The third and final trap is called the 'Path of God'. Indy comes to an opening in the side of a sheer cliff face but there appears no way to reach the other side.

"You must believe boy, you must believe," Indy hears his father struggling to whisper.
Indy steps out over what seems like a sheer drop. His faith is rewarded as a camouflaged bridge is revealed, leading him to a cave where he is greeted by a knight.

The knight is the last of the three brothers who had sworn an oath to guard the Grail and has been on duty for 700 years.

The cave walls are lined with chalices. "Which one is it?" demands Indy.

"You must choose. The true grail will bring you life... the false grail will take it from you," the knight answers.

Donovan bursts into the cave with Dr Schneider.
"Let me chose," says Schneider as she passes Donovan a golden cup encrusted with jewels. He swigs from the cup and begins ageing rapidly until his body decays and crumbles into dust.

"He chose poorly," the knight says. Indy then picks a simple wooden jug. "That's the cup of a carpenter," he says before filling it with water and drinking. Nothing happens and Indy knows he has chosen the true Grail!

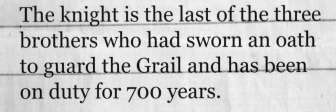

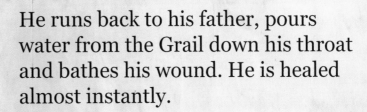

He runs back to his father, pours water from the Grail down his throat and bathes his wound. He is healed almost instantly.

Elsa grabs the grail and attempts to escape but the walls collapse and the ground caves in. The Grail falls down one of the gaps in the rock and Elsa refuses to let it go. Indy tries to save her but she slips from his grasp and falls to her doom.

Indy is then in the same position, with the same dilemma. Should he keep hold of the Grail and risk falling to his doom? Indy's father pleads with him and Indy leaves the Grail, grabs his father's arm and clambers to safety.

Indy and the other conquering heroes leave the canyon with the blessing of the knight. They set off on horseback as another adventure is complete.

INDIANA JONES

Congratulations! You are doing very well, but do you have what it takes to complete another round of tricky questions?

1. In which castle is Indy's father held captive?
Answer:

2. What is Donovan's first name?
Answer:

3. By what means of transport do Indy and his father escape from Berlin?
Answer:

4. Which infamous historical figure signs the Grail diary?
Answer:

5. What is the name of the group who have sworn to defend the Holy Grail?
Answer:

6. In which Italian city do Indy and Marcus meet Dr Schneider?
Answer:

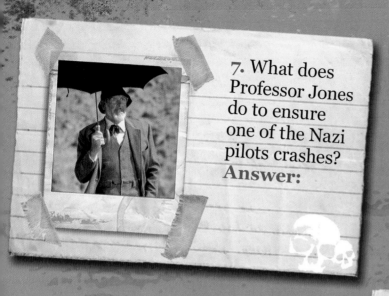

7. What does Professor Jones do to ensure one of the Nazi pilots crashes?
Answer:

8. Who chooses the chalice that Donovan drinks from?
Answer:

9. What does Indy's father send to him in the post from Venice?
Answer:

10. In what type of building do Indy and Elsa discover underground tombs?
Answer:

11. What are the Nazis burning in Berlin when Indy and his father arrive?
Answer:

12. What is the name of Indy's friend who accompanies him on the trip to Venice?
Answer:

13. How does Professor Jones usually refer to his son?
Answer:

14. Who shoots Indy's father in the stomach?
Answer:

SPOT THE DIFFERENCE

Study these two pictures from *Last Crusade*. There are five differences, will you be as eagle-eyed as Indy and be able to spot them all?

LAST CRUSADE WORD SEARCH

Try to find the words listed below in this special *Last Crusade* word search. The words can be written horizontally, vertically, backwards and diagonally in both directions.

A	W	U	K	S	L	T	C	P	H	R	Y
V	J	W	Y	H	H	R	S	L	D	F	Q
O	O	U	H	G	E	D	C	Q	K	I	Y
S	O	W	I	O	F	C	X	D	X	T	Y
K	L	N	J	R	G	F	D	A	A	E	H
E	K	I	L	L	I	R	S	C	O	T	T
J	E	T	X	K	N	B	A	H	Y	U	O
E	Q	E	W	E	X	Z	Z	I	T	F	X
C	A	E	D	D	E	S	B	T	L	C	N
I	N	L	O	D	F	O	H	Y	U	I	I
N	A	B	N	Y	B	S	X	Z	Q	N	L
E	T	T	O	M	R	D	F	S	A	C	R
V	F	Y	V	S	S	S	R	R	N	A	E
V	B	A	A	A	N	N	A	L	Z	D	B
L	A	A	N	V	S	R	P	I	Q	N	C
Z	A	I	O	U	D	F	A	J	C	Q	X
Q	U	V	C	N	L	J	P	C	P	T	U
W	T	R	V	N	H	S	D	P	N	O	O
S	A	S	C	H	N	E	I	D	E	R	Q
M	G	A	I	O	O	V	A	E	X	S	E
O	Z	A	L	S	R	I	M	K	E	F	A
P	K	L	N	I	L	E	P	P	E	Z	T

- ☐ DONOVAN
- ☐ SCHNEIDER
- ☐ GRAIL
- ☐ KNIGHT
- ☐ BERLIN
- ☐ MARCUS
- ☐ ZEPPELIN
- ☐ VENICE

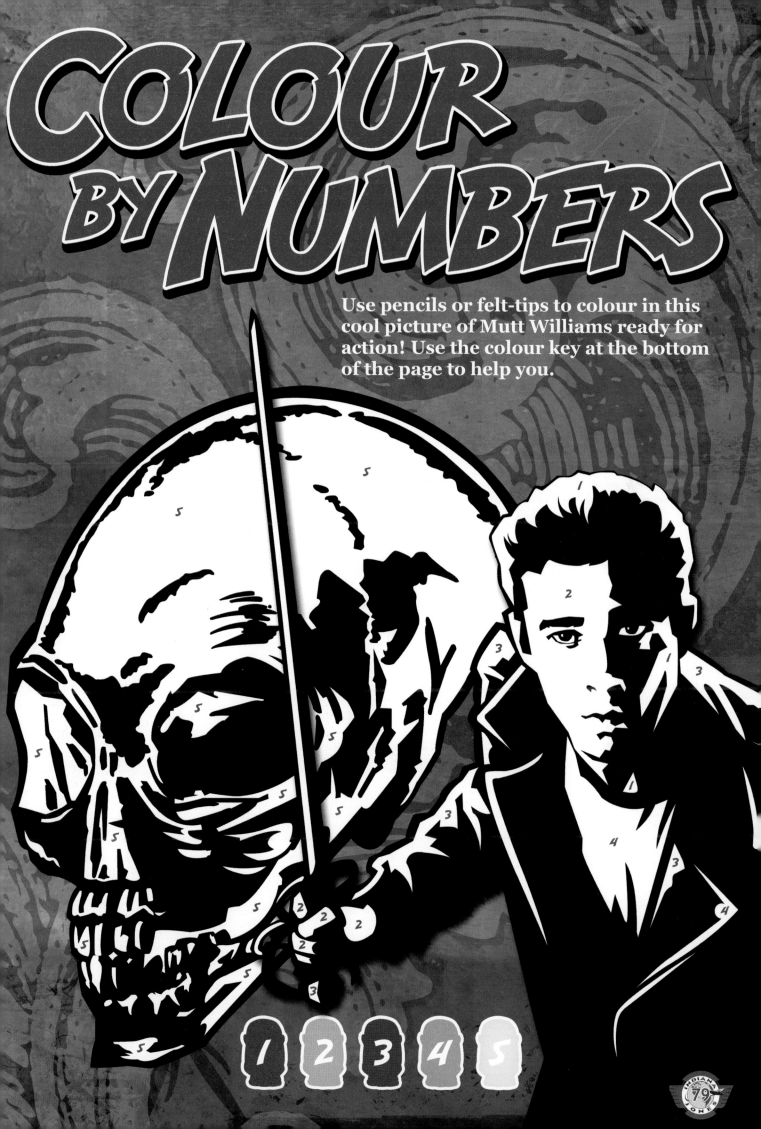

COLOUR BY NUMBERS

Use pencils or felt-tips to colour in this cool picture of Mutt Williams ready for action! Use the colour key at the bottom of the page to help you.

10 QUESTIONS
ABOUT LOCATIONS

Is your geographical knowledge as good as Indy's? Pick one of the three options for each question.

1. In which US city does Indy live and teach?

a) Bedford
b) Philadelphia
c) Chicago

2. In which country is Pankot Palace?

a) Morocco
b) India
c) Sri Lanka

3. In what country is the city of Cairo?

a) Egypt
b) Algeria
c) Tunisia

4. In which German city does Indy reclaim his father's Grail diary from Dr Elsa Schneider?

a) Munich ☐
b) Berlin ☐
c) Dortmund ☐

5. In what US state is the military base that Indy and Mac are taken to?

a) Texas ☐
b) Florida ☐
c) Nevada ☐

6. To which South American country does Dr Jones fly with Mutt Williams in search of Marion and Harold Oxley?

a) Argentina ☐
b) Bolivia ☐
c) Peru ☐

7. What is the name of the river that Indy, Marion, Mutt, Mac and Ox travel down, negotiating three fierce waterfalls along the way?

a) Amazon ☐
b) Nile ☐
c) Mississippi ☐

8. In which Italian city do Indy and Marcus meet Elsa Schneider for the first time?

a) Rome ☐
b) Venice ☐
c) Milan ☐

9. In which country does Indy make a deal with crime boss Lao in return for a diamond?

a) China ☐
b) Japan ☐
c) Thailand ☐

10. Which country is Indy's rival archaeologist, Belloq from?

a) Germany ☐
b) Spain ☐
c) France ☐

KINGDOM OF THE CRYSTAL SKULL

[PROFILE]

Marion
Ravenwood

Indy's former fiancée comes back into his life years after they separated following Indy's decision to call off their wedding. Born in 1909, the daughter of famous archaeologist and treasure-hunter, Abner Ravenwood, Marion first met Indy in 1925. Marion is independent, stubborn and ready to put herself at risk to defend her friends and family.

[PROFILE]

Mutt
Williams

Marion's son Mutt is young and impetuous. He always has a point to prove and is ready to challenge anybody who disrespects him or his mother. After quitting school early, Mutt now mends bikes to make a living. He shares Indy's love of adventure.

Harold
Oxley (Ox)

[PROFILE]

Harold Oxley was born in Leeds, England, in 1887 and studied archaeology at University with Marion's father, Abner Ravenwood. Oxley also met Indiana Jones whilst in Chicago but broke off their friendship after Indy left Marion in the lurch. Ox is obsessed with a crystal skull of an ancient legend and is willing to travel the globe and put his life at risk to locate it.

George
McHale (Mac)

Englishman George McHale, usually known as Mac, has known Indy for many years. An archaeologist, Mac met Indy during the Second World War when the pair worked for military intelligence. Mac has saved Indy's life on more than one occasion! He loves gambling and the good life and has a passion for gold treasure and anything that can make him money. This greed often causes him to make poor decisions.

Dr Irina
Spalko

[PROFILE]

Dr Spalko grew up in a small mountain village in the Ukrainian Soviet Socialist Republic. An intelligent and forceful woman, Spalko's quest for knowledge saw her join the Soviet secret police where she became a respected and successful officer who won many awards. A cold-hearted woman, she trained in many forms of combat. Will her obsessive and relentless quest for knowledge ultimately be her downfall?

Antonin
Dovchenko

[PROFILE]

Antonin Dovchenko is a physically imposing Russian Colonel who acts as Dr Spalko's right-hand-man. Dovchenko enjoys making others suffer and is extremely adept at inflicting pain on his enemies. A loyal servant of the Soviet Union, Dovchenko dominates his men and strikes fear into the hearts of most of his rivals.

The Last Adventure?

INDIANA JONES
and the
KINGDOM OF THE CRYSTAL SKULL

A convoy of army vehicles heads along the Nevada state highway to a top-secret military base. It's 1957 and Indiana Jones has been taken hostage during an archaeological dig with his friend Mac in Mexico. The vehicles stop in front of a hanger and a soldier forces Indy out of a car. His blindfold is removed and as Indy's eyes struggle to adjust to the brightness he hears the soldiers talking.

"Russians!" he whispers.
"This won't be easy," Mac replies.

A tall, pale woman with a sword hung at her side addresses the colonel who has hold of Indy.

"At ease, Antonin Dovchenko," she says.
She introduces herself as Dr Irina Spalko, originally from the state of Ukraine in the Soviet Union.

"I intuit things. I know them before anyone else, and what I do not know, I learn," she adds.
"And what I need to know now is in here," she says tapping her finger on Indy's head.

The hanger doors open to reveal thousands of wooden crates, stacked into high piles.

"This is where your government hides its military treasures," Spalko shouts. She describes a highly magnetised rectangular storage container she is looking for.

Indy asks for the gunpowder from the soldiers' guns and hand grenades. He throws the powder through the air and along the ground and the draw of the magnetism reveals the location of the box.

As Spalko and her men are transfixed by the body found inside the casket Indy uses his whip to grab one of the soldier's guns and then throws a rifle to Mac. But when Indy looks across at Mac he realises his old friend has sided with the Russians.

"Drop the gun," orders Dovchenko. "Whatever you say," Indy replies. He drops the gun to the floor so it shoots a bullet into a soldier's foot. As Indy battles with a chain-wielding Dovchenko in an underground bunker he spots an explosively charged mechanical chair attached to rails.

Indy and Dovchenko shoot forward at break-neck speed, their faces stretched back by the powerful G-forces. The chair comes to a halt and as Dovchenko collapses Indy flees.

EXPRESS

A nearby town is eerily silent. It contains plastic mannequins posing as human families, inside life-sized houses. A warning siren sounds and a countdown begins. Indy has stumbled across a testing area for a deadly atomic bomb.

Indy runs inside a house and notices a large refrigerator with a lead lining. He clambers inside just before the big bang. The fridge is thrust high into the air before bouncing into the desert.

A US Army patrol rescues Indy who is interrogated by two FBI officers. He explains how Russians kidnapped him and that his old friend Mac turned on him. But the FBI believe Indy could be a spy for the Russians – and he is fired from his job at Marshall College!

As Indy is about to leave town on a train a young man on a motorcycle revs along the platform.

"Are you Doctor Jones?" the young man shouts. "Are you a friend of Harold Oxley?"
"What about him?" Indy asks.
"They're gonna kill him," the young man replies.

The motorcyclist introduces himself as Mutt Williams. He explains Harold Oxley is in trouble and talks about a crystal skull Oxley has become obsessed with. Mutt says his mother received a letter from Oxley six months earlier. It had been sent from Peru and said he'd found a crystal skull.

"It's believed that whoever finds the missing skull and returns it to Akator's temple will be granted control over its power," Indy says.

Mutt explains that his mother and Ox are held captive in Peru. He fears that if his mother cannot persuade Ox to reveal the location of the skull, both of them will be killed.

"Ox said that the skull has psychic powers and that he was taking it to a place called Akator," says Mutt.

Indy explains that Akator is a giant lost city made of gold and that legend speaks of a native tribe called the Ugha who built the city with the help of the gods.

A conquistador called Francesco de Orellana, known as the Gilded Man because of his love of gold, disappeared in the Amazon rain forest in 1546 whilst searching for Akator.

Indy deciphers the riddle Ox has written on a letter handed to him by Mutt. It's written in an ancient language called Koilhomoa.

"Follow the lines that only the gods can read," he says "but what could Ox mean?" he asks himself. "Of course... he means the Nazca lines!" Indy shouts.

Indy explains the Nazca lines are ancient patterns etched into the desert floor in Nazca, Peru. They can only be viewed from above, referring to the line that 'only the gods can read them'.

Indy and Mutt fly to Peru and discover Ox had staggered into Nazca a few months earlier, shouting and ranting like a wild man. Police took him to the local asylum but Ox was later taken away by a group of men.

He left behind markings on his cell walls. The word 'return' has been written in many languages. Ox must have become obsessed with returning the skull to Akator.

Indy notices a drawing etched in the layers of sand and dust on the ground and realises it points to a cemetery or sacred burial ground, Orellana's resting place.

Indy and Mutt go in search of the conquistador's grave and discover a hidden entrance to an underground temple.

Before they can enter the eerie surroundings of the tomb, Indy and Mutt come under attack from several cemetery warriors. As the thunder and lightening crashes out of the sky, the warriors appear from empty graves and blow poisoned darts at Indy and Mutt, but Indy manages to fight them off. "You're a teacher?" Mutt asks. "Part time," Indy replies with a smile.

There are bundles of bodies that have been preserved for hundreds of years in wrappings. One is the Gilded Man, Orellana.

Indy lifts away Orellana's clothing and discovers a huge elongated crystal skull. Ox had taken the skull to Akator and then returned it. But why had he returned it?

As they emerge from the darkness of the tomb they are met by Mac and the Russians who take Indy and Mutt prisoner and transport them by boat up the Amazon to a camp in Ilha Aramaca.

Indy is tied to a chair inside a large tent. Dr Irina Spalko enters. "How fortunate our failure to kill you, Dr Jones," she says. "You survive to be of service to us once again."

She describes the crystal skull as a weapon the Russians can use to strike fear across the United States and the world by channelling its power against people's minds. Indy now realises Oxley had put the skull back because he knew the Russians were looking for it!

"That skull is no mere deity carving," Spalko says. "It was not made by human hands."
"Saucer men from Mars?" Indy mocks.

"The legends about Akator are all true," Spalko insists. "It was a city of supreme beings with advanced technology and paranormal abilities."

She then unveils a body taken from Nevada and shows Indy the preserved remains of what appears to be an alien. She pulls away the flesh around the head to reveal a skull of pure crystal.

Two Russian soldiers drag Harold Oxley into the tent. He is disorientated and appears to be in a trance.

"What have you done to him?" Indy demands.
"We haven't done a thing, it's the skull," Mac answers.

Spalko picks up the skull and explains how the crystal stimulates an undeveloped part of the human brain, opening a psychic channel. She claims Oxley lost his mind by staring into the eyes of the skull for too long.

"We believe you can get through to him after you have done the same," she says to Indy who is forced to stare into the eyes of the skull.

Spalko speaks of the skull's powers and says the Russians could place their thoughts into the minds of American leaders and make US soldiers attack on their command. "We'll be everywhere at once, more powerful than a whisper," she says.

Indy is entranced as the skull's eyes give out a bright blue light. His upper body jerks uncontrollably.

"You will speak to Oxley and lead us to have Akator!" Spalko screams. Indy refuses.

Spalko orders the soldiers to take him outside. Mutt's mother Marion is dragged out of another tent. "Indiana Jones," she says with a smile, "it's about time you showed up!"

Indy recognises his old flame Marion Ravenwood and realises she is Mutt's mother.

Ox begins repeating the name, "Henry Jones Junior" as his memory appears to be returning.

"To lay their just hands on that Golden Key," Ox says, "that ope's the Palace of Eternity,"

"Ox, you've got to tell us how to get to Akator, or they're going to kill Marion," Indy pleads.

"Through eyes that last I saw in tears, here in death's dream kingdom," Ox mumbles as Indy notices he's rotating his right wrist in a writing movement.

"Get me paper. Something to write with," Indy shouts at Spalko. Oxley begins to draw. "Three times it drops on the way down," Ox whispers.

Indy realises the drawings are directions. The drawing of the great snakes means the Amazon river and the directions point along the river Sono.

Mutt sees his chance and punches one of the guards, allowing the group to escape into the jungle.

But Indy and Marion get stuck in quicksand and begin to sink rapidly. Mutt and Ox run for help. As they are sinking Marion reveals that Mutt is Indy's son.

Mutt returns with what appears to be a large rope or vine. He throws it to his mother and drags her free. He then throws it towards Indy, who hesitates, realising the vine is in fact a snake!

"I hate snakes!" Indy shouts. With the sand just inches from his chin, Indy pretends the snake is a rope and grabs it so he can be pulled to safety.

Mac arrives accompanied by soldiers, brought by Ox in his disillusioned state. The four are loaded into an army van but a squabble starts as Indy and Marion discuss their break-up and Mutt.

"Why did you bother to tell me now?" Indy demands.
"Because I thought we were going to die," she replies.
"Not yet!" Indy shouts, kicking Dovchenko in the back.

Indy jumps onto a jeep containing Ox, knocks Mac out with a single punch and overpowers the other soldiers.
"Indy, Indy, I'm CIA!" claims Mac, protesting he's actually a double agent.

Spalko's jeep pulls alongside and a soldier throws her the skull. Marion pulls her vehicle alongside as Mutt and Spalko begin a swordfight. Mutt grabs the skull but loses possession and is knocked from the jeep by the high-kicking Spalko.

The battle continues on a narrow road along the edge of a sheer cliff face. Both jeeps crash over huge humps, which turn out to be the nests of flesh-eating ants. Indy eventually knocks down Dovchenko whose body is dragged into a nest by the ants.

Marion picks up Indy and Ox in the jeep, which is shaped like a boat. She drives straight off the cliff face but the vehicle clips a large tree on its way down, slowing its speed, and it lands safely in the river below.

"Three times it drops," Oxley says out loud.
Indy realises he's talking about a massive waterfall! They miraculously survive the waterfalls before abandoning the jeep.

"Through eyes that last I saw in tears," says Ox, clutching the crystal skull.
"The golden vision reappears!" Mutt shouts as he realises what Ox has seen. Looking up at a large rock face shaped like a skull Mutt guesses they have to go through the eyes to reach the city of gold.

The group is ambushed by spear-throwing local tribesmen who chase them down the steep temple steps. Oxley gets the skull out of the bag and shows it to the tribesmen who slowly back away in fear.

The adventurers arrive at an abandoned city. Indy decides Ox has been here before but couldn't get into the temple and so took the skull back to the cemetery.

"To lay their just hands on that Golden Key that open's the Palace of Eternity," Ox again says to Indy as he pours sand into his palm.

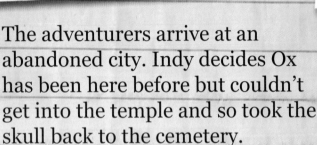

Ox walks around the walls that are surrounded by murals of different heads. He feels every head before finding one that moves. Indy slams a large rock on it and millions of grains of sand ooze from the wall. Four pillars rise together forming a tower and the ground collapses beneath the adventurers.

As they walk further into the temple Mac secretly drops a flashing red device on the floor. It's not the first one he has dropped and it's clear he's leaving them so Spalko can follow the trail.

Indy and his group enter another large room filled with many antiques and treasures. Ox holds the skull aloft in front of him and walks towards a large ornate, red and gold doorway. The skull appears to be glowing as Indy takes it from his friend.

Indy sees a gap in the door and holds the skull against it. The skull is the key that slowly opens the doors to reveal a huge room filled with 13 thrones. On top of each throne is a crystal skeleton of a massive extra-terrestrial being.

One throne is missing a skull. Ox prepares to return the crystal skull to its body - but Mac draws his gun!

"So what are you, a triple agent?" Indy asks.
"Nah, I just lied about being a double," Mac answers as Spalko enters the burial chamber.

"Look at them! Imagine what they could tell us," she says, approaching the skeleton missing its skull. The skull flies out of her hand and attaches to the body. The being appears to come to life.

Oxley approaches and begins speaking in a strange language.
"He's speaking Mayan," Indy says.
"He says the being wants to give us a big gift."
"Tell me everything you know, I want to know everything," Spalko says to the being.

The crystal skulls begin to vibrate and hum. The eyes of the skeletons glow brighter. The walls of the room crumble and rotate as the thrones whiz round, making loud humming noises.

"What are they, spacemen?"
Mutt asks.
"Inter-dimensional beings, in point of fact," Ox replies, having snapped out of his trance.

The ceiling cracks and what appears to be a huge spaceship hovers over them, shining a bright light into the temple.

"What the hell is that?"
Marion asks.
"A portal," Ox replies, "A pathway to another dimension."
Indy drags Ox and the others out of the temple.

Spalko remains. She wants the knowledge of the inter-dimensional beings. All the beings come together to form one individual that has the appearance of an alien.

"Enough, cover it," Spalko shouts, pain etched across her face.
Mac refuses to leave with the others and is sucked into the portal. The rest of the temple crumbles as Indy leads the escape.

Spalko struggles as the being overloads her mind with information. Her eyes catch fire and her body disappears in a ball of flames.

LIVE FOR ADVENTURE
INDIANA JONES
1935
FORTUNE AND GLORY

Indy and his adventurers are caught at the bottom of a well as gallons of water are released from the temple. The water lifts them to the top where they clamber up a cliff to watch Akator crumble.

The huge silver portal that looks like a flying saucer flies off causing a huge canyon to appear.

"Where did they go, space?" Indy wonders.
"Not into space. Into the space between spaces," Ox replies.
"Why is this known as the city of gold?" asks Mutt.

"The Ugha word for gold translates as 'treasure'," Indy answers.
"But their treasure wasn't gold. It was knowledge."

The four return home. Indy is reinstated at the university and he and Marion finally get married, with Mutt as best man.

As the three walk back down the aisle together following the wedding, a gust of wind blows the church door open, ushering Indy's famous hat on the ground at Mutt's feet.

Mutt picks it up, but Indy claims it back and walks out of the church with his beautiful bride on his arm.

INDIANA JONES

Excellent! You are almost there. Just one last test to go but will you finish it in time to escape? Let's find out...

1. What is the name of the city of gold?
Answer:

2. To which South American country do Indy and Mutt travel to try and save Marion and Ox?
Answer:

3. Which state within the Soviet Union is Dr Spalko from?
Answer:

4. What is the name of the ancient people who worshiped the inter-dimensional beings as gods?
Answer:

5. When he says, "Three times it drops," what is Ox talking about?
Answer:

6. What is Mutt's surname?
Answer:

7. What does Indy use for shelter when he gets caught up in a nuclear test blast?
Answer:

8. Which river do the adventurers travel down?
Answer:

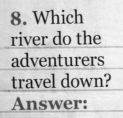

9. What is the full name of the Russian colonel who is Spalko's right-hand man?
Answer:

10. Which country are both Mac and Oxley from?
Answer:

11. What does Mutt use to save Indy and Marion from the quicksand?
Answer:

12. By what other name is Francesco de Orellana known?
Answer:

13. How many inter-dimensional beings are found on thrones in the burial room of the temple?
Answer:

14. What is the real treasure of the city of gold?
Answer:

SPOT THE DIFFERENCE

Study these two pictures from *Kingdom of the Crystal Skull*. There are five differences, will you be as eagle-eyed as Indy and be able to spot them all?

KINGDOM OF THE CRYSTAL SKULL
WORD SEARCH

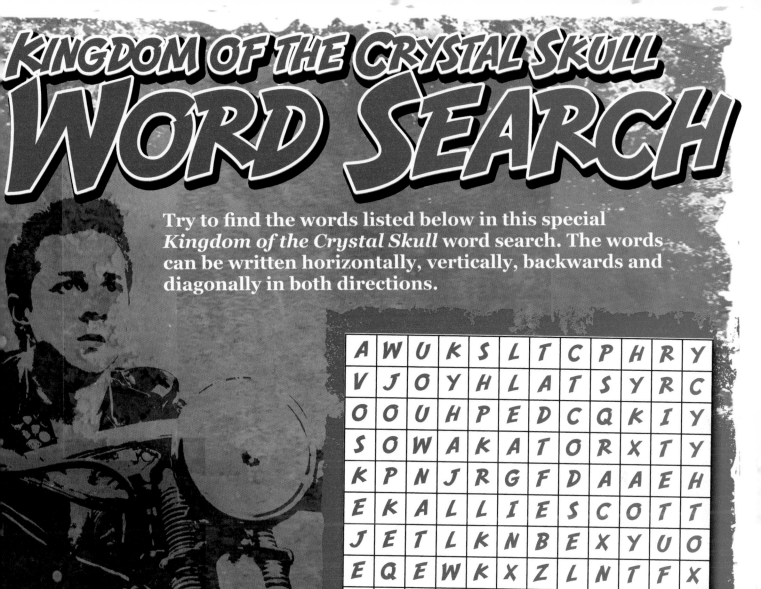

Try to find the words listed below in this special *Kingdom of the Crystal Skull* word search. The words can be written horizontally, vertically, backwards and diagonally in both directions.

A	W	U	K	S	L	T	C	P	H	R	Y
V	J	O	Y	H	L	A	T	S	Y	R	C
O	O	U	H	P	E	D	C	Q	K	I	Y
S	O	W	A	K	A	T	O	R	X	T	Y
K	P	N	J	R	G	F	D	A	A	E	H
E	K	A	L	L	I	E	S	C	O	T	T
J	E	T	L	K	N	B	E	X	Y	U	O
E	Q	E	W	K	X	Z	L	N	T	F	X
A	A	E	D	D	O	E	B	T	L	C	N
D	J	L	L	D	Y	O	H	Y	U	I	L
N	A	B	L	Y	K	S	X	Z	Q	N	L
W	T	T	P	V	R	D	F	S	A	C	R
S	F	Y	E	S	L	S	R	R	N	A	T
V	B	A	R	A	N	N	A	L	Z	D	T
L	A	A	U	V	U	R	P	I	Q	N	U
Z	A	I	O	Y	D	F	A	J	C	Q	M
Q	D	O	V	C	H	E	N	K	O	T	U
W	T	R	V	N	H	S	D	P	T	O	O
S	T	U	P	H	N	F	N	D	O	O	Q
M	G	A	G	O	O	V	A	E	X	S	E
O	Z	O	L	H	R	I	M	K	A	L	A
P	K	L	I	A	A	T	P	I	E	Z	T

- ☐ SPALKO
- ☐ CRYSTAL
- ☐ OXLEY
- ☐ DOVCHENKO
- ☐ MUTT
- ☐ PERU
- ☐ UGHA
- ☐ AKATOR

HERO OR VILLAIN?

From the pictures of the following characters can you remember which are Indy's friends and which are his enemies?

Willie Scott
Friend☐ Enemy☐

Belloq
Friend☐ Enemy☐

Marion Ravenwood
Friend☐ Enemy☐

Mutt Williams
Friend☐ Enemy☐

Dr Irina Spalko
Friend☐ Enemy☐

Short Round
Friend☐ Enemy☐

Antonin Dovchenko
Friend☐ Enemy☐

Toht
Friend☐ Enemy☐

Mola Ram
Friend☐ Enemy☐

10 QUESTIONS
ABOUT KINGDOM OF THE CRYSTAL SKULL

How much do you remember about Indy's latest adventure? Pick one of the three options for each of the questions.

1. What is the full name of Indy's long-term friend Mac?

a) John MacIntosh ☐
b) George McHale ☐
c) Andy McCarthy ☐

2. From which Soviet Union country is Dr Irina Spalko?

a) Hungary ☐
b) Poland ☐
c) Ukraine ☐

3. By which name is the lost city made of gold also known as?

a) Pankot ☐
b) Mola Ram ☐
c) Akator ☐

4. What is the name of the river that Indy has to follow to where it joins the Amazon?

a) Sono ☐
b) Mono ☐
c) Serano ☐

5. What is the first name of Marion's father?

a) Abraham ☐
b) Alan ☐
c) Abner ☐

6. When Indy and Marion are sinking in the quicksand, what does Mutt throw at them to help them escape?

a) A rope ☐
b) A snake ☐
c) A spear ☐

7. After fighting Indy, a swarm of what devours Dovchenko?

a) Ants ☐
b) Bees ☐
c) Scorpions ☐

8. When Harold Oxley says "three times it drops." What is he referring to?

a) A spaceship ☐
b) The sun ☐
c) A waterfall ☐

9. What is the name of the tribesmen that confront Indy, Marion, Ox, Mutt and Mac before they enter the temple where the crystal beings are located?

a) Thuggees ☐
b) Munga Bugah ☐
c) Ugha ☐

10. How does Harold Oxley describe the alien-like beings that fly away in the spaceship-like portal?

a) Inter-dimensional beings ☐
b) Extra-terrestrial beings ☐
c) Crystal Aliens ☐

INDIANA JONES
19 57
MUTT

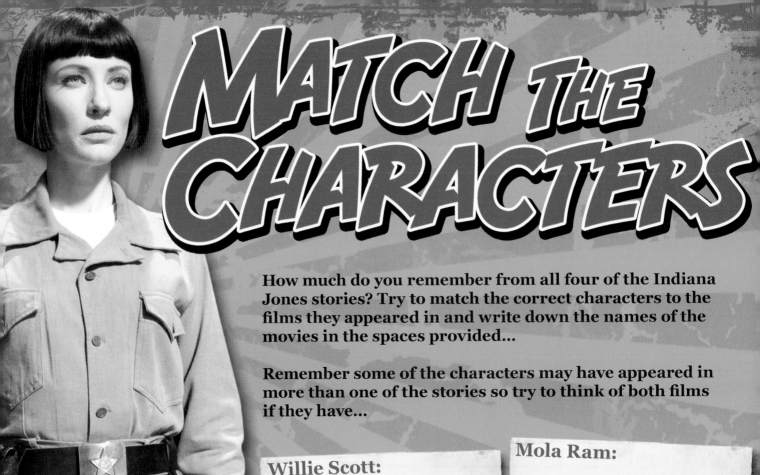

MATCH THE CHARACTERS

How much do you remember from all four of the Indiana Jones stories? Try to match the correct characters to the films they appeared in and write down the names of the movies in the spaces provided...

Remember some of the characters may have appeared in more than one of the stories so try to think of both films if they have...

Willie Scott:

Mola Ram:

Marion Ravenwood:

Henry Jones Senior:

Mutt Williams:

Dr Harold Oxley:

Marcus Brody:

Short Round:

Sallah:

Dr Irina Spalko:

Belloq:

Mac:

TRUE OR FALSE?

Using your knowledge of all four films, work out which of the following 10 statements are true and which are false...

1. Indy hates snakes
True ☐　False ☐

7. Marion Ravenwood's father is called Harold 'Ox' Ravenwood
True ☐　False ☐

2. Indy's father calls him 'Junior'
True ☐　False ☐

8. The penitent man will not pass
True ☐　False ☐

3. The god the Thuggee cult worship is called Sali
True ☐　False ☐

9. Indy's father Henry has had a life long obsession with the Crystal Skull
True ☐　False ☐

4. Antonin Dovchenko is a German spy
True ☐　False ☐

10. Indy is Mutt Williams' father
True ☐　False ☐

5. Willie Scott is a professional singer
True ☐　False ☐

6. Mutt Williams rides a motorcycle
True ☐　False ☐

ANSWERS

Page 28
Spot The Difference

Page 52
Spot The Difference

Page 76
Spot The Difference

Page 100
Spot The Difference

Page 30
Raiders of the Lost Ark
Word Search

A	W	U	K	S	L	C	C	P	H	R	Y
V	J	F	Y	E	S	A	I	O	S	W	Q
O	O	U	H	K	E	D	C	Q	K	O	Y
P	O	I	N	A	G	C	X	D	L	T	Y
Q	L	K	J	N	G	F	D	L	A	E	H
R	T	K	J	S	P	U	E	N	D	M	A
S	E	T	X	K	N	B	G	H	Y	U	L
A	Q	S	W	E	X	Z	Z	J	B	F	L
O	R	H	U	D	E	S	B	M	V	C	A
J	N	K	B	D	F	O	I	Y	U	I	S
Z	A	L	G	Y	B	N	X	Z	Q	N	G
E	T	N	L	M	M	D	F	S	A	C	U
P	F	K	N	T	S	S	R	R	N	N	O
V	B	A	G	N	A	T	A	K	S	D	E
L	K	G	N	A	R	P	W	Q	N	C	Q
B	N	U	O	S	D	F	H	J	C	Q	X
S	U	V	J	N	L	A	P	E	N	T	U
P	T	D	V	G	H	S	D	K	N	O	O
B	I	K	J	D	C	O	P	S	D	W	Q
H	G	Y	I	D	O	A	A	E	X	V	E
T	D	I	E	T	R	I	C	H	E	F	A
S	K	L	C	A	A	U	O	O	O	D	J

Page 53
Temple of Dome
Word Search

A	W	U	K	S	L	C	C	P	H	R	Y
V	J	W	Y	M	A	R	A	L	O	M	Q
O	O	U	H	B	E	D	C	Q	K	I	Y
S	O	I	S	O	T	C	X	D	X	D	Y
E	L	K	J	R	G	F	D	A	A	E	H
E	W	I	L	L	I	E	S	C	O	T	T
G	E	T	X	K	N	B	G	H	Y	U	O
G	Q	S	W	E	X	Z	Z	J	M	F	X
U	A	H	U	D	E	S	B	A	V	C	L
H	N	O	B	D	F	O	H	Y	U	I	E
T	A	R	G	Y	B	A	X	Z	Q	N	G
E	T	T	L	M	R	D	F	S	A	C	K
P	F	Y	N	A	S	S	R	R	N	A	O
V	B	A	J	A	A	N	A	L	L	D	E
L	A	H	N	V	I	R	P	I	Q	N	C
Z	A	R	O	S	D	F	A	J	C	Q	X
T	U	V	A	N	L	J	P	C	N	T	U
O	T	D	V	K	H	S	D	P	N	O	O
K	I	K	J	D	N	O	P	S	D	W	Q
N	G	A	I	O	O	A	A	E	X	V	E
A	Z	A	L	S	R	I	S	K	E	F	A
P	K	L	C	A	A	U	O	O	O	D	J

Page 77
Last Crusade
Word Search

A	W	U	K	S	L	T	C	P	H	R	Y
V	J	W	Y	H	H	R	S	L	D	F	Q
O	O	U	H	G	E	D	C	Q	K	I	Y
S	O	W	I	O	F	C	X	D	X	T	Y
K	L	N	J	R	G	F	D	A	A	E	H
E	K	I	L	L	I	R	S	C	O	T	T
J	E	T	X	K	N	B	A	H	Y	U	O
E	Q	E	W	E	X	Z	Z	I	T	F	X
C	A	E	D	D	E	S	B	T	L	C	N
I	N	L	O	D	F	O	H	Y	U	I	I
N	A	B	N	Y	B	S	X	Z	Q	N	L
E	T	T	O	M	R	D	F	S	A	C	R
V	F	Y	V	S	S	S	R	R	N	A	E
V	B	A	A	A	N	N	A	L	Z	D	B
L	A	A	N	V	S	R	P	I	Q	N	C
Z	A	I	O	U	D	F	A	J	C	Q	X
Q	U	V	C	N	L	J	P	C	P	T	U
W	T	R	V	N	H	S	D	P	N	O	O
S	A	S	C	H	N	E	I	D	E	R	Q
M	G	A	I	O	O	V	A	E	X	S	E
O	Z	A	L	S	R	I	M	K	E	F	A
P	K	L	N	I	L	E	P	P	E	Z	T

Page 101
Kingdom of the Crystal Skull **Word Search**

A	W	U	K	S	L	T	C	P	H	R	Y
V	J	O	Y	H	L	A	T	S	Y	R	C
O	O	U	H	P	E	D	C	Q	K	I	Y
S	O	W	A	K	A	T	O	R	X	T	Y
K	P	N	J	R	G	F	D	A	A	E	H
E	K	A	L	L	I	E	S	C	O	T	T
J	E	T	L	K	N	B	E	X	Y	U	O
E	Q	E	W	K	X	Z	L	N	T	F	X
A	A	E	D	D	O	E	B	T	L	C	M
D	J	L	L	D	Y	O	H	Y	U	I	L
N	A	B	L	Y	K	S	X	Z	Q	N	L
W	T	T	P	V	R	D	F	S	A	C	R
S	F	Y	E	S	L	S	R	R	N	A	T
V	B	A	R	A	N	N	A	L	Z	D	T
L	A	A	U	V	U	R	P	I	Q	N	U
Z	A	I	O	Y	D	F	A	J	C	Q	M
Q	D	O	V	C	H	E	N	K	O	T	U
W	T	R	V	N	H	S	D	P	T	O	O
S	T	U	P	H	N	F	N	D	O	O	Q
M	G	A	G	O	O	V	A	E	X	S	E
O	Z	O	L	H	R	I	M	K	A	L	A
P	K	L	I	A	A	T	P	I	E	Z	T

Pages 26 and 27
Quiz 1
1. Nepal
2. Marshall College
3. French
4. Cairo
5. Snakes
6. Inside a basket
7. Toht
8. The Ark of the Covenant
9. Professor Abner Ravenwood
10. Colonel Dietrich
11. Sallah
12. Belloq
13. To close her eyes and not look at it
14. A US Government warehouse

Page 29
Who am I?
1. Short Round
2. Toht
3. Walter Donovan
4. Sallah
5. Willie Scott
6. Dr Irina Spalko
7. Harold 'Ox' Oxley
8. Marion Ravenwood
9. Mac
10. Mutt Williams

Page 31
Who said What?
"I can't go to Pankot, I'm a singer!"
– **Willie Scott**

"If you listen to me, you'll live longer"
– **Short Round**

"Don't call me Junior!"
– **Indiana Jones**

"Indy, why does the floor move?"
– **Sallah**

"Fortune and glory kid, fortune and glory!" – **Indiana Jones**

"I intuit things. I know them before anyone else, and what I do not know, I learn." – **Dr. Irina Spalko**

"Well what can I say Jonesy? I'm a capitalist, and they pay." - **Mac**

"To lay their just hands on that Golden Key that ope's the Palace of Eternity."
– **Harold 'Ox' Oxley**

"Indiana Jones. Are you still leaving a trail of human wreckage behind you everywhere your go?"
– **Marion Ravenwood**

"The healing power of the grail is the only thing that can save your father now." – **Walter Donovan**

Pages 32 and 33
10 Questions about Indiana Jones
1. c / 2. c / 3. b / 4. c / 5. c / 6. a / 7. b / 8. c / 9. a / 10. a

Pages 50 and 51
Quiz 2
1. Obi-Wan
2. Round
3. Mayapore
4. Nurhachi, the first Emperor of the Manchu dynasty
5. Chattar Lal
6. A diamond
7. Kali
8. Left
9. Elephant
10. Zalim Singh
11. Delhi
12. India
13. Monkey brains
14. Sankara

Pages 56 and 57
Villains 10 Questions
1. b / 2. c / 3. a / 4. b / 5. c / 6. c / 7. b / 8. c / 9. b / 10. a

Pages 74 and 75
Quiz 3
1. Brunwald Castle
2. Walter
3. Zeppelin airship
4. Adolf Hitler
5. The Cruciform Sword group
6. Venice
7. He disrupts a flock of birds
8. Dr. Elsa Schneider
9. His Grail diary
10. A church
11. Books
12. Marcus Brody
13. Junior
14. Walter Donovan

Pages 80 and 81
10 Questions on Locations
1. c / 2. b / 3. a / 4. b / 5. c / 6. c / 7. a / 8. b / 9. a / 10. c

Pages 98 and 99
Quiz 4
1. Akator
2. Peru
3. The Ukraine
4. The Ugha
5. A waterfall
6. Williams
7. A refrigerator
8. The Amazon River
9. Andrei Dovchenko
10. England
11. A snake
12. The gilded man
13. 13
14. The treasure of knowledge

Page 103
Hero or Villain?
Willie Scott – Friend
Belloq – Enemy
Marion Ravenwood – Friend
Mutt Williams – Friend
Dr Irina Spalko – Enemy
Short Round – Friend
Antonin Dovchenko – Enemy
Toht – Enemy
Mola Ram – Enemy

Pages 104 and 105
10 Questions Kingdom of the Crystal Skull
1. b / 2. c / 3. c / 4. a / 5. c / 6. b / 7. a / 8. c / 9. c / 10. a

Page 106
Match the Character
Willie Scott – *Temple of Doom*

Mola Ram – *Temple of Doom*

Marion Ravenwood – *Raiders of the Lost Ark* and *Kingdom of the Crystal Skull*

Henry Jones Senior – *Last Crusade*

Mutt Williams – *Kingdom of the Crystal Skull*

Dr Harold Oxley – *Kingdom of the Crystal Skull*

Marcus Brody – *Raiders of the Lost Ark* and *Last Crusade*

Short Round – *Temple of Doom*

Sallah – *Raiders of the Lost Ark* and *Last Crusade*

Dr Irina Spalko – *Kingdom of the Crystal Skull*

Belloq – *Raiders of the Lost Ark*

Mac – *Kingdom of the Crystal Skull*

Page 107
True or False?
1. True / 2. True / 3. False / 4. False
5. True / 6. True / 7. False / 8. False
9. False / 10. True